PRAISE FOR
ICE AND STONE
AND MARCIA MULLER

*Recipient of the Private Eye Writers of America
Lifetime Achievement Award
And the Mystery Writers of America
Grand Master Award*

"Muller undoubtedly remains one of today's best mystery writers." —Associated Press

"One of the world's premier mystery writers."
—*Cleveland Plain Dealer*

"Muller's McCone set the standard for fictional women detectives; after 35 installments, the detective's character has not diminished but continues to evolve and grow and meet all challenges head-on. A must-read for Sharon McCone fans; the series should also be explored by any fan of strong women detectives."
—*Library Journal*

"Will turn any reader into a nail-biter...deftness in writing combined with the lead character's passionate morality and willingness to fight for the underdog are what have made this series successful for its long run...delivers a fast, intense, thought-provoking read." —*New York Journal of Books*

ICE AND STONE

ICE AND STONE

Marcia Muller

GRAND CENTRAL
PUBLISHING

NEW YORK   BOSTON

For Bill, with love

Acknowledgments

Many thanks to:

Molly Friedrich, my agent, for her constant encouragement.

Elizabeth Kulhanek and Mari C. Okuda, for their editing skills.

Laura Neditch, for insight on the extreme northern parts of our state.

Melissa Ward, for the Feather.

Alison Wilbur, for laughter in the face of adversity.

Yvonne Russo, for her thoughtful feedback on the portrayal of Indigenous people and culture in this novel. Any remaining inaccuracies are my own.

And my readers, who have kept Sharon McCone in business for over forty years.

The County of Meruk and the Meruk Nation are fictional, but the California locales bear similarities to many communities within our state. Any misrepresentations are my own. No characters depicted have any relationship to the living or the dead.

This novel was written in better times, before the corona virus and racial unrest racked our country. Therefore, no mention of either has been made. There is, however, plenty of commentary about the inequities that have finally moved us to take control and begin our journey back toward normalcy.

ICE AND STONE

In the Land of Ice
and Stone

Meruk is the smallest and least known of California's fifty-nine counties. Roughly triangular in shape, it abuts the Oregon border at its narrowest, most mountainous point and slopes south into wide grassland near the Lassen County line. The Meruk Nation, or "mountain people," after whom the county is named, are peaceable and gentle; they are concerned with preserving their environment and practicing their arts; although they are the smallest nation in the state, their weavings, pottery, and basketry have spread far from their ancestral grounds.

Their calm productivity is severely at odds with their surroundings. The land, while spectacular, is often hazardous; the climate can be harsh in the extreme. The events of its bloody and cruel history are well documented in the few historical accounts of the tribe—violent events that were not instigated by the Meruk Nation but by the white people who came seeking gold, land, lumber, and numerous other riches.

Today Meruk County is relatively peaceful. The lumber industry was phased out long ago, due to its distance from the dog-hole shipping ports at the coast. Tourism is minimal, thanks to miles of badly maintained and winding roads as well as a paucity of lodging places. Large cattle ranches cover the county's southern territory and provide the tax money that keeps the budget in the county seat of Ames balanced. People scratch out an existence by farming small plots or fishing on the Little White River or working the ranches.

Before I traveled north, I had little knowledge of the Meruk. Having been adopted and raised as Scotch-Irish, and not having discovered my Shoshone roots until middle age, I wasn't familiar with many of the nations. But after the case I'd gone to Meruk County to pursue, I would become all too familiar with the victims of vengeance, racial injustice, and profound ignorance.

SATURDAY, JANUARY 5

4:13 p.m.

From its rim at the side of Fisher's Mill Road, the deadfall looked treacherous: sand-colored boulders, felled trees, tangled dead branches, moraines of rock and sediment spilling down to the river below. I hefted my cumbersome backpack, looked dubiously at the walking stick that my guide, Allie Foxx, had provided to help me keep my balance.

Yeah, sure—I'll probably still end up on my ass.

Allie was already halfway down the slope. She made a hurry-up sign to me. I closed my eyes and started off.

Closing my eyes was not the smartest thing I'd ever done: my work boots skittered over a patch of stones, a branch whopped me on the forehead, and I came to rest leaning against a birdlimed outcropping.

When I looked down the slope, I saw Allie had turned her back. She was probably hiding laughter. Her tribe, the Meruk, I'd read, did not believe in ridiculing others.

Well, I had to admit I must look ridiculous: clumsy in my overstuffed cold-weather clothing, red faced and sweating in spite of the icy wind. But dedicated—oh yes.

I'd been hired the previous week by the Eureka-based Crimes against Indigenous Sisters organization to investigate why two Native women had been murdered in Meruk County over the past three months as well as look into many prior disappearances. The cases were not localized: Indigenous women have long been victims of mysterious crimes in areas from Arizona to the far reaches of Canada, from the Sierra Nevada to the Pacific. But Meruk and its surrounding counties—Del Norte, Tehama, Siskiyou, and Modoc—had experienced an ominous uptick in such crimes, and CAIS wanted to know why. So did I.

I straightened, set my backpack more firmly on my shoulders, and started off again. This time the going was easier and, except for a couple of near falls, I made it upright to where Allie was now waiting on the bank of the Little White River. To her left the water flowed free from under an ancient arched stone bridge, but to her right the river became choked by more downed trees, dead grasses, and boulders. I slid toward her on a pebbled patch of ice.

She smiled, her white teeth a sharp contrast to her brown, weathered skin. "We'll make a cross-country tracker of you yet, Sharon."

"Cross-country catastrophe is more like it."

"Nah, you just need a little more practice." Her expression became serious. "This cell phone is for you. As I mentioned before, none work here except those signed up with the local provider, and, at that, the reception is spotty. You may have to go into the village to make any calls."

"Thanks. I take it Internet service is just as bad."

"Worse, I'm afraid. You won't have a vehicle for

a couple of days, but the village is walkable, and I've arranged with my brother who has a car dealership in the county seat to have a Jeep delivered to you. The shack is fully stocked, and anything you need, just give a call. You have your keys?"

"Yes. And my instructions and my lists."

"Sorry to sound like an overprotective mama, but I was one for a lot of years. Be careful on that ledge under the bridge, it's slippery. Once you're on the other side, you turn left—"

"Yes, Mom."

"And in an emergency, you'll—"

"I know."

"Okay. This is where I leave you. The killer, or killers, might recognize me, given the publicity the organization's been getting. I'll put as much distance between us as possible." She squeezed my arm, turned, and walked quickly uphill.

I was on my own.

The narrow ledge under the bridge *was* slippery, but I had the walking stick for balance. Even through my thick boots I could feel the iciness of the water, and sharp stones poked against their soles. The arching bridge wall felt clammy and smelled of mold. Rustling sounds accompanied my passage, and I thought of bats.

And then I was out on the far side. The light was fading, so I flicked on my small flash before proceeding. I scrambled left up the mud-slick slope, past a jumbled pile of rocks and there—

There it was.

The old abandoned shack belonging to the Sisters was built of redwood that had weathered to a dull silver gray. Its windows were nailed shut with many sheets of plywood and crisscrossing timbers; tattered black shingles lay loose on its roof, some littering the ground. The single door was secured by a rusted chain and an odd-looking padlock. It seemed as if no one had entered it in decades.

But I knew better.

The padlock was difficult, even though Allie had given me a demonstration when she'd handed me the key. One prong of the key had to be inserted at an angle, another pushed up from below. When I pulled, nothing happened; I removed and reinserted the key, pressed harder, pulled again. There was a faint click, and the staple released. I removed the padlock and the chain, pulled the door open, and stepped inside.

Under other circumstances I would have expected dust, cobwebs, and stale odors, but instead a pleasant, flowery scent came to my nostrils. Air freshener. I shone my light around the single room. Two lanterns sat on the big braided rug. I fumbled in my pocket for matches, lit one.

The light from the lantern was dim; I was pleased with that, even though Allie had told me that every chink between the old boards had been caulked to prevent telltale leakage. I set my pack down and looked around.

The structure had been built in the mid-1980s by a man who had inherited the land and hoped to turn it into a retreat for recovering alcoholics, but the extremes of weather and difficulty of hauling in construction supplies had defeated him, and he'd died—sadly, an alcoholic himself—in the early 2000s, willing the property to the Sisters, who had befriended him and nursed him in his final illness. They'd maintained the cabin as well as they could, but they'd been working against great odds. And now it seemed they'd worked hard at reclaiming it for me.

To my right, under the windows, was a bunk topped with an air mattress, a sleeping bag, and a big, fluffy pillow; to the left a tiny bathroom with a chemical toilet and small sink had been partitioned off from the rest of the room. Two jugs of water, foodstuffs, and other supplies were stowed beneath a wide shelf.

I eyed the comfortable-looking bunk. I was exhausted. Early that morning I'd flown my Cessna 170B from its base at Oakland Airport's North Field to a tiny paved strip at Bluefork over in Modoc County. The strip belonged to Hal Bascomb, one of my husband Hy's flying buddies, who had been sworn to secrecy about my presence in the area and had provided the loan of one of his three dilapidated Quonset hut hangars to shelter the plane. After we stowed the plane, Hal gave me a hand up into his Jeep. He looked good: sun browned and golden haired in spite of the time of year. Long ago he and Hy had worked together on some dodgy jobs in Southeast Asia, and they had been friends ever since. Now Hal claimed he was taking it easy, that running the strip in Bluefork was his retirement. But I could see that same steely look in his eyes that I occasionally glimpsed in Hy's. People in certain pursuits never quite retire.

Allie had met us on the outskirts of the nearby village of Aspendale in her Land Rover, and after a short drive she and I had arrived in Saint Germaine. An unincorporated and fairly unpopulated area, named after a long-abandoned monastery on the far side of the river, Saint Germaine was where the fatal attacks on two Indigenous women had occurred over the last three months. I'd have to—

Table that until tomorrow, McCone. You're too tired to think clearly now. Put on your sweats, crawl into that bunk, and get some sleep.

SUNDAY, JANUARY 6

2:27 a.m.

One of the windows above the bunk was propped open about five inches, but in a way that wouldn't be visible from outside. Before I'd wrapped myself in the sleeping bag and blankets—so new they still had the store tags attached—I'd arranged my super-sensitive sound-activated tape recorder on the sill. In case anyone—or anything—came around, it would alert me and record their actions. The promise of snow was in the air, and sheets of ice groaned where they'd formed at the bend of the river. I'd drifted off to the sound of loose stones clattering in strong current.

Louder noises broke my sleep. I pushed up on one elbow, brushed my hair off my face. Heavy footsteps and men's voices, two of them, coming down the hill. I checked my watch, then the recorder, to make sure it was working. Took my .38 Special from where I'd wedged it between the air mattress and its frame, lay back against the pillows, and waited.

The footsteps came around the cabin and stopped. One of the men gasped, and I could hear him breathing laboriously. The other said, "Christ, Gene, you're gonna have a coronary if you don't lose some of that flab."

"Screw you." Gene gasped again; it took him a moment to get the hacking under control.

"Well, listen to yourself," the other said.

"Son of a bitch tells us to leave the ranch in weather like this, he's trying to kill us. What's with him, anyway?"

"Probably more of his fancy guests coming."

"What's that to do with us?"

"Don't know. He pays good, though."

"Not good enough for us to pay for a room in one of those fleabag motels."

"It's good money for these parts, though."

"For these parts, but nowhere near city rates."

"So take yourself off to a city, get a bigger-paying job, and then try to live on it at city prices."

"I done all right in the cities back in the day. I bet if I went down to Sacramento, San Francisco—"

"You'd starve."

"Look, I worked in L.A. once—"

"Yeah, once. When you was a lot younger. And thinner. A lot better lookin' too."

"Come on, Vic. You're not in such great shape yourself. If you were, we might've gotten lucky today."

"What does being in shape have to do with it? We never even seen so much as a goddamn deer."

"All right, all right."

"Man, I'm not looking forward to sleeping on the cold ground. Why don't we break into the shack?"

I tensed, glanced at the shack's door. Had I secured it properly? I cradled the .38 to my chest, waited.

"Nah, it's too much trouble. Besides, it belongs to one of the tribes. We don't want any hassle with their police—or the feds."

"Jesus Christ, I'm so sick of Injuns. All the names they got for 'em too. 'Native Americans.' 'Redskins.' 'Indians.' What's it matter?"

"Well, if you was one it might matter to you."

"But I'm not. I'm a one hundred percent red-blooded American boy."

"*Red* blooded?"

"Well, fuck you!"

Rustling noises, as if the men were laying out sleeping bags.

Long silence, then Gene's voice asked, "You want some of this? It's pretty good whiskey."

"Yeah, sure."

"Kinda takes the sting outta the cold, don't it?"

"Does. Look, Gene, I don't know about you, but what I'm gonna do now is crawl into my sleeping bag. Come dawn we're outta here, be at the ranch by eight."

"Probably have to work the whole damn day."

"So what? We get paid tomorrow."

"Get paid, go buy us a couple more bottles, maybe play a little blackjack at the casino, then back to work again next day. What a life!"

"It ain't so bad. Not lately, you got to admit that. Wouldn't be better anywhere else, that's for sure, even if you had someplace to go."

"I got places I could go."

"Sure you do. Just keep on telling yourself that."

Silence, then, except for the sounds of the men settling into their sleeping bags. I curled up, breathing in small intakes and exhalations.

"Vic?"

"What now?"

"The old man—he's crazy, ain't he?"

"Hell, I don't know."

"He must be. I mean—"

"Shut up, Gene."

"I mean—"

"Shut up!"

Gene snorted, shifted around, then fell silent.

A little time passed. Then Vic said in a plaintive tone, "Hey, I didn't mean what I said."

"Huh?"

"About you having no place to go. Even after that mess with the girl over in Reno, you could—"

"Leave it, man. She was nothing but a tramp, and she left town good and quick. Besides, I asked you never to talk about Reno. Stuff is what it is. Just let it be."

Silence again.

Two minutes more, and then:

Gene: It's goddamn cold here. Maybe we shoulda gone up to the other place. At least we could've slept inside there.

Vic: Too far away. And even colder and windier. You got any of that antifreeze left?

Gene: Got some, yeah.

Vic: You sharing?

Gene: Do I have a choice?

Drinking sounds, followed by a loud belch. After a few minutes, Gene said, "You asleep?"

"I will be, if you ever shut up."

"But—"

"I said if you ever *shut up!*"

Silence, except for the drone of an airplane in the distance. Small jet, I thought, as I pulled my covers higher. I was still on edge but feeling reasonably safe, so I passed the time thinking about what little I'd learned from the men's conversation. An old man on a nearby ranch had sent them away. Who was he? And what did the men do at the ranch? Couldn't be anything important; they didn't sound like the brightest bulbs in the box. Maybe they were security guards. Long ago I'd worked in the field; I knew what security guards sounded like, and these two fit my recollections. But why would someone need guards in this godforsaken outpost?

A hundred scenarios would dance in my dreams if I couldn't tamp down my imagination, and I'd wake exhausted. I closed my eyes, tried to quiet my thoughts. It didn't help much, and when I did drop off and dream, I saw shadowy extraterrestrials with tentacles and huge eyes on stalks creeping down the ridge toward the shack.

I swatted one on the nose, and they went away.

6:49 a.m.

Groans, grunts, and mumbles. The men were getting up.

> *Gene:* Shit! My back hurts.
> *Vic:* Keep thinking about the dough we're gonna collect.

Gene: Yeah, I can use it for my spine surgery.

Vic: Why are you always so negative?

Gene: Just my nature, I guess.

Vic: Well, screw your nature. Let's get outta here, get to the ranch. I'm hungry.

Gene: You're always hungry.

Vic: *You're* the one with the gut.

7:17 a.m.

After I was sure the men wouldn't return, I got up, pulled on jeans, boots, and a wool shirt, and went outside. The snow that I'd expected had come at some point, but it must have been a brief flurry, leaving only a light dusting on the rocky ground. I could see vague outlines of where the men had been lying. I went over and studied the area.

An empty pint bottle of Four Star, a cheap blended whiskey. A pile of used tissues—I'd heard one of them hacking and wheezing as they got up. Cigarette butts—Marlboros. A Bic lighter. That was all. Nothing that might identify either of them.

Back inside the shack, I checked my image in the mirror from my purse. In this light my face had a grayish pallor and my eyes were dark circled. After years of wearing my black hair at shoulder length, I'd recently let it grow; without combing it, I caught it up in a rubber band and let it straggle down my back. As I looked at my reflection, a shiver touched my shoulder blades. Now I superficially resembled one of the murder victims, Samantha

Runs Close, whose photo I'd studied over the past week.

I bundled up in a raggedy parka that I'd found among the things the Sisters had left for me and stepped outside again with the walking stick in hand. After replacing the lock and chain on the door, I headed north along the Little White River to the area where the bodies of the two victims had been found.

The morning was cold, the sky mostly clear now, but the chill air still held the scent of snow. The sun was barely cresting the eastern hills that separated Meruk from Modoc County, a strong pink glow.

The river wound through pines and aspens, many of them dead or dying from the West's seven-year drought, which had partially broken last year. Unfortunately, the torrential rains that followed had produced catastrophic mudslides; I climbed over their leavings as I kept to my easterly path.

All the time I listened. To the forest sounds of unseen animals large and small rustling in the undergrowth, but mostly for the steps of the most dangerous animal of all—man. I'm always alert for danger in unfamiliar surroundings, especially on an investigation of the type that had brought me here.

I kept my free hand on the .38 inside the parka's deep pocket. I have mixed feelings about firearms. From a professional's standpoint, I'm damned happy to own one; I don't carry often, but when I do, it's for a good reason; a few times, doing so has saved my life—others' lives too. Even though I've killed in self-defense with my gun, the memories of those times live on in my nightmares. I fully support more stringent regulations on the sale and licensing of firearms, and I despair that they've yet to be enacted.

Once I had a high school friend—a well-meaning but naïve naval officer—who, worried about his wife's safety while he was on a long deployment, bought her a .22-caliber automatic at a pawnshop. He loaded it, put it in her bedside table drawer before shipping out to Alaska. Three months later she was dead, the victim of a burglar whom she'd confronted with the weapon; he'd easily taken it away and shot her because her husband hadn't instructed her in the critical act of taking the safety off.

I wish we lived in a world where weapons of any kind weren't easy to obtain or even necessary. But in this world, wishes don't count.

The river meandered through the forest, in some places running fast, in others spreading out into still pools. Birds—from melodious songsters to harsh crows—provided a continual chorus. A long-tailed woodpecker went to work on a ponderosa pine, and a gimlet-eyed hawk swooped overhead, scanning the ground for prey.

At one point the river crested a rise, then cascaded into a small waterfall. I stopped and leaned on an outcropping, drinking from my water bottle and getting my bearings. I'd been headed due east, but ahead of me the river took a sharp bend to the north, and through the thick vegetation I could make out a jumble of dark stones. The remains of St. Germaine Riviere, the abandoned monastery where the bodies of the two murdered women had been found.

The monastery, Allie Foxx had told me, had been founded in 1910 by a little-known order of Catholic monks dedicated to educating the Natives of the area. They met with little success and considerable hostility, and when the structure burned to the ground in 1951, arson was suspected. The few remaining monks had fled, and the church had displayed little interest in the property, which now had been reclaimed by the forest, a monument to the failure of the faiths and races to coexist.

A wooden footbridge leading to the ruins had collapsed into the river, but heavy planks had been laid down beside it. Tattered, weathered yellow crime-scene tape fluttered in the light breeze, and on a wide section of open ground nearby I spotted ruts and gouges where a rescue helicopter had landed. Some of the blackened buildings had collapsed in huge scattered chunks, now covered by moss and birdlime.

I studied the ruins. A few walls still stood, others had been totally leveled. Decaying timbers stretching the walls' entire length had caved into a stone foundation marking a large structure—perhaps a chapel. Heaps of slate from the roof littered the ground, and old, tough vines wound over them. Tall weeds swayed in a sudden breeze, and the heavy limbs of nearby oak trees moved, groaning and casting shadows across the whole area. Suddenly I felt as if I'd come upon a long-untended graveyard.

But there were no graves here—only the reminders of two violent deaths.

I tested the sturdiness of the planks over the river, then crossed them. Stopped and tried to match what I was seeing to the crime-scene photographs the Sisters had provided. Samantha Runs Close had been lying over a massive granite slab. The other victim, Dierdra

Two Shoes, had been found farther in among the rubble. Both had been shot in the head. Neither had been sexually assaulted. The bodies had been discovered by a pair of bird hunters.

I prowled among the ruins, though I doubted I'd find any overlooked evidence of what had happened here. The murders—which occurred in early December—had been investigated by the county sheriff's department and tribal police from the nearby Meruk reservation. But the sheriff's department's resistance to the Sisters' and tribal cops' request to see their files troubled me, as did the general assumption among the populace described to me by the Sisters—that the deaths had been isolated incidents, over and done with, never to be solved and therefore best forgotten.

No, dammit, you don't ignore or forget such horrific crimes. They must be investigated, they must be brought to a conclusion.

It was only nine o'clock, but the sky was darkening. Gravid cumulus clouds moved slowly in over the hills to the east. More snow on the way, maybe heavier this time. Still I lingered, reluctant to leave.

Certain places, especially those where traumatic or violent events have occurred, have a distinctive feel. As the dark gathered, obscuring ordinary details, I was sensing that phenomenon here. Not through auditory hallucinations or Technicolor flashes, strong scents or unusual temperatures—those are special effects for Hollywood movies. Rather the place held a troubling aura: sorrow, regret, loss, a rending, as if some essential part had been irretrievably ripped from its whole.

I walked among the ruins for a long time.

10:30 a.m.

I was midway down the river trail when I found the silver pendant.

A glint of metal caught my eye, and I crossed the trail toward it. A tree had been uprooted, and in the disturbed ground lay a charm in the shape of a feather that had many more intricate feathers incised upon it. At its top was a ring through which a light blue silk thread was strung; the thread had been broken off about four inches above the ring.

A pendant, I thought. Fallen from someone's neck, perhaps pulled off in a struggle.

I took out one of my plastic baggies and slipped the pendant into it, then put the bag in my jeans pocket. On the right of the path, between two jagged boulders, was an area where the damp earth looked trampled. I moved over for a close look at the rocks. On the leeward one, free of a dusting of snow, were crusty brownish smears that could be blood.

Samantha Runs Close and Dierdra Two Shoes had both been shot in the head and, according to the county medical examiner, died where they'd been found. I'd seen no signs of a struggle at either location, but there were definitely some here. A third murder in this area that the authorities had missed? It was entirely possible.

I took out my cell and snapped a few pictures of the disturbed earth and bloodstains. The light here was bad. I glanced up at the sky; the snow clouds had moved in closer, driven by high winds. I hurried down the trail, anxious to get back to the protection of the shack.

11:45 a.m.

I needn't have hurried. By the time I reached the shack, the storm had bypassed the area, the winds whipping the snow-filled clouds to the southeast. I struggled with the difficult padlock. It stuck, started to give, stuck again, and finally yielded.

After chaining the door and turning on one of the lanterns, I sat on the bunk to examine the silver feather. It was an unusual charm, probably handcrafted, with the initials HH on its back. Made by a local artisan, who might recognize it and remember to whom he or she had sold it? Maybe someone in Aspendale? No reason I couldn't go there this afternoon.

Of course, how to deal with showing the pendant was problematic. If it was evidence of a struggle, I didn't want to make myself a target. Finally I decided I would wear it with the shabby clothing and parka that the Sisters had provided as camouflage, on the off chance somebody would recognize and comment on it. I'd have to be doubly on my guard; after all, I suspected it had last been worn by a victim of violence.

The path to Aspendale was easy to follow, compared to the trail along the river. It crossed Fisher's Mill Road, where Allie had led me through the deadfall the other day, then wound downhill through forest. There were patches of ice on the ground, and a couple of times I didn't notice them until I slipped and righted myself. Sunlight filtered through the branches, making the snow patches glitter; birds again took up their chorus, and I saw a buzzard sitting up high, spreading its huge wings to dry. I narrowly avoided plunging into slick runoff that coursed down a slope.

As I walked, I made a mental to-do list: wander about the village, allowing as many people as possible to see the pendant; stop in shops, making a few small purchases and trying to strike up conversations. Keep my ears open and senses attuned.

Undercover work like this was something I hadn't done in a long time. In San Francisco I had a high profile that prevented it. I was used to making appointments with the principals in a case, walking in, and asking my questions. This process was more delicate and much more challenging.

The village appeared around a curve in the path: the main street was no more than three blocks long, with side streets bisecting it. Some of the buildings were false fronted, as in old Western movies; others were cement block; some were redwood plank and no sturdier looking than the shack. A few beater cars were parked in front of a bar called Billiards 'n Brews; a structure that looked like a former church advertised available office space; there was a Good Price Store, a Fine Food Mart, a Valero gas station, a lumberyard, a hardware store, and a hair salon called Gigi's Curls. There wasn't a soul in sight.

First the Good Price Store: overheated, with a smell of disinfectant. Short aisles crammed with all manner of merchandise: beach toys were shelved between lawn mowers and snow shovels; baby clothes hung limply next to plastic flowers; candy mingled with housewares. In a couple of long aisles the shelves were mostly empty. There was one register up front, unmanned. A bell above the door had tinkled as I entered, and I pretended interest in a display of greeting cards till someone appeared.

A thin, ponytailed young Native woman with a wide smile approached me. She said, "That's a new line we just got in. Nice, I guess, if you're sentimental."

"I'm not." I turned and touched the pendant so she had a full view of it.

"Oh," she exclaimed, "you've got one of Henry Howling Wolf's pieces! That's a particularly beautiful one."

"I think so too."

"Did he make it for you personally?"

"Ah, no. I ordered it by mail. I actually wanted to see him and thank him for sending it to me, but I've lost his contact information. Do you have it?"

"Sure." She pulled out an old Rolodex from under the counter and wrote it down on a slip of paper. As she handed it to me, she asked, "You're new around here, aren't you?"

"Yes."

"Welcome. I'm Sasha Whitehorse, by the way."

"I'm Sharon McNear. Glad to meet you." The cover story had been suggested by the Sisters; the name was my choice—close enough to my own so I'd respond to it quickly.

"Thank you. Are you a tourist? We don't get many this time of year."

"No. Actually, I'm a journalist." It was a cover story one of the Sisters had suggested to me.

"A journalist? Are you here to write about the murders?"

I feigned innocence. "What murders?"

"Oh, I guess you wouldn't know. A couple of girls got killed here a while back."

"Really? Did the police catch who did it?"

"Not yet." Sasha fidgeted and changed the subject. "Where are you staying?"

"At a motel near Bluefork. The E-Z Rest." Hal had asked the owner to vouch for me.

"It's kind of a hot sheet."

"I suspected as much. It'll do for a while, though."

"Will you be here long?"

"That depends on what there is to see and do. What I'll be writing is a travel-oriented piece."

She laughed. "Then you won't be here long. Look where we're at." She swept her arm around—at the store, at the town, at everything, I supposed. "There's nothing here, never has been. I stay because I've got no place else to go. You know how it is."

No place to go. Like Gene, according to his friend Vic.

"I do, but tell me anyway."

"Well, it's a poor county. The minimum wage in this state is due to rise to fifteen bucks soon, but I make five, and I'm lucky to get it. The housing sucks—me and my boyfriend and another couple live in a drafty barn at Hogwash Farm and pay the old guy who owns it in chores. There's nothing to do."

"Are people afraid to go out because of the murders?"

A door closed at the rear of the shop. The woman cast a nervous look back there. "That's the man who owns this place. Please go before he comes in!"

"Why? I don't understand."

"Please! He doesn't like me talking too long with the customers!"

I went.

1:15 p.m.

Outside the store I tried to call Henry Howling Wolf, but there was no answer. Heeding hunger pangs, I stopped in at the Fine Food Mart for a sandwich, some chips, and a Coke. The middle-aged man at the register was closed faced and rung up my purchases silently. He glanced at the pendant but displayed no recognition.

I said, "How's your day going?"

"Okay."

"Think it's going to snow again soon?"

"Nope." He turned his back and studied the newspaper on the shelf behind him. The *San Francisco Chronicle*, probably two or three days old—proof that no matter how far you travel, you can't escape the media in one form or another.

Back on the street, foot traffic had picked up. Women and men were shedding the heavy scarves that had been bundled around their necks and turning their faces up to the pale sun. A few smiled or nodded at me; most seemed indifferent. Ahead I spied a bulky man with his jacket flipped over his shoulder. He had dark hair going gray at the temples and walked with a pronounced waddle. A shorter, thinner, blond man carrying a paper bag joined him outside the Good Price Store.

"About time, Vic," the other man said.

I quickly moved past them and halted in a narrow alley between buildings. Gene and Vic. Last night, they'd seemed like not-very-bright good ol' boys, but in the light of day, their bloodshot eyes glittered and their mouths turned down as they pushed around other pedestrians, who drew back in response.

Not good ol' boys at all.

The two of them climbed into a beat-up old pickup and drove off. I went back to the main street. The air was warmer now, and the ditches beside the badly paved road ran with melted snow. The Owl Cafe and Gigi's Curls had CLOSED signs in their windows, and the gas station—an honor-system, pump-your-own type—was deserted too. Even the hardware store was closed. Didn't people in this town ever work?

1:44 p.m.

I walked back through the village and turned off on a trail that a sign indicated led to Watson's Pond, which Allie Foxx had mentioned as a quiet place that she enjoyed. The path was partly overgrown and little used, and it ended less than a mile later at a scum-covered body of water with a couple of old wooden benches on the grass nearby. Not the most scenic place to have my picnic and think, but so what? I took out my sandwich and settled down to consider the lives of the two victims.

Dierdra Two Shoes had been promiscuous, according to those who knew her—including her mother.

Mrs. Lagomarsino had told Allie, displaying neither regret nor sadness, "That girl had every chance in the world. A couple of her men were very rich and powerful. They would have given her anything." The mother had refused to name the men.

Samantha Runs Close had fit her name. An activist for Indigenous women's rights, she'd clawed, scratched, and fought at demonstrations throughout the state. Before I'd come up here, I'd asked Hy, an avid supporter of environmental causes, if he'd heard of her. He'd said, "Every dedicated activist knew and respected Sam. She would demonstrate against anything, but finally focused on Native rights. I guess she fought for them until her dying day."

3:01 p.m.

When I got back to town, I called Henry Howling Wolf's number again. This time he answered, abruptly, on the first ring. He seemed disappointed when I identified myself, as if he'd been expecting to hear from someone else. I told him I had acquired one of his pendants and would like to talk to him about it. He brightened some, then invited me to come to his house.

The house was a white prefab on the outskirts of Aspendale, surrounded by a grove of small fir trees that had the super-green needles of new plantings. A homemade sign in the front yard read H. H. DESIGNS. Henry Howling Wolf was a short, slightly obese young man with black bowl-cut hair that covered his

eyebrows. He stared at the pendant, seeming somewhat distracted, as he ushered me into his home.

The room was a long one, with a seating area near
a woodstove and a work space at the rear. There were
various tools hanging neatly from a pegboard, a long
bench, a stool, and several machines whose purpose I
couldn't begin to imagine.

Henry asked, "You wouldn't be a buyer, by any
chance? My inventory's sold out, but there's always
next year."

"Sorry, no, I'm a journalist. I'd like to talk with
you about your work—and your success."

"Always glad to talk," he said, although he didn't
sound glad at all. He motioned for me to sit down.
"What can I tell you?" His gaze was jumpy, moving
quickly to a telephone on a side table and then to me
and the pendant again.

Before I told him how I'd gotten it, I decided to
reduce his tension. Over the course of my career, I'd
been subjected to many interviews of the "How did
a girl like you end up in this business?" variety. They
were as numbing as a heavy dose of Valium.

"Tell me how you got started," I said.

He motioned at the shop area. "A few years ago, I
was thinking of quitting this and going to school to
learn refrigerator mechanics. I'd even enrolled at the
technical college, but then my first big order came in.
Ever since, I've been overwhelmed with work."

"Who do you primarily sell to?"

"Souvenir companies. H. H. Designs makes pendants, key rings, pins, and any other number of
whatchamacallits that are all available at airports, bus
stops, and convenience stores nationwide." His smile

was self-deprecating, but beneath it I sensed a well-deserved pride.

"Good for you."

"Well, some of the stuff is downright tacky—not the great Indigenous art I'd aimed for—but the people who buy them like them."

The phone rang. Henry jumped up, but it immediately stopped.

I said, "Is there a problem, Mr. Howling Wolf? Anything I can help you with?"

"I don't see how. It's my girlfriend, Sally Bee. She's missing. She's been gone for almost forty-eight hours."

"Gone. You mean she left you?"

"I don't know what's happened. Sally's a photographer. She went out in the morning two days ago to get some shots of a place where she was having difficulty getting the right light. When she didn't come back, I called around to our friends, thinking she might have stayed with one or another of them. She does that sometimes. But I've heard nothing." His big hands dropped heavily to his sides.

"Do you think this pendant might be hers?"

He leaned forward, studying it. "I don't know. It could be."

"Could you tell by examining it?"

"No. I made only three with that design, all identical—one for a woman who died four years ago, the other for a friend who moved to Portland two years ago. It could belong to one of them. How did you get it?"

"I found it in the woods, on the trail to the old monastery."

"That's where Sally was going to get her photographs! You...you didn't find anything else around there?"

"No, nothing. Just the pendant. Mr. Howling Wolf, I don't mean to be unkind, but since you're not sure it's Sally's, I'd like to keep it for the time being. When she comes back and if it is hers, of course I'll return it. I'll be here for several days."

He didn't put up an argument, merely drew a deep, steadying breath and then said, "Sally, she's a talented woman. A photographer. She's already published a couple of books on native California plants with a small press in Berkeley. She came here with the idea of doing a book on the Meruk. Her work complemented mine, and we used to talk about getting away someplace else where we could live quietly and practice our arts. But now she's gone. Just...*gone*."

"Did she take anything with her?"

"Only the camera she was using that day. She has several others, but they're still here."

"You didn't hear or see her leave?"

"No. I was upset the night before and I'd taken a sleeping pill."

"Upset?"

Again he hesitated, then, seemingly glad to have someone to tell his problem to, replied, "The county sheriff, Noah Arneson, had been coming around asking if we had business licenses, that kind of crap. But we knew what he was doing."

"And what was that?"

"Arneson hates Natives. Especially successful ones. He's been trying to make us leave the county, but we got our backs up and stayed. I wish to God we hadn't."

"You think the sheriff had something to do with Sally's disappearance?"

"I don't know. But it's funny that he pestered us almost daily before she left and hasn't bothered me since."

It was interesting, I thought, that Henry hadn't mentioned the murders. Maybe he didn't want to believe that his Sally might be another victim.

I asked him for a photograph of Sally Bee, saying I might need it for the article I was writing, and—surprisingly—he didn't have one. "A lot of photographers don't like having their pictures taken, I guess," he explained. We talked some more; he said they'd experienced no harassment except for Sheriff Arneson's.

God, I wished the investigation weren't leading toward corrupt law enforcement. Cases like that are hard to prove and incur the wrath of the public.

And they can turn ugly. Very ugly.

5:15 p.m.

There was nothing more to be done in town today, and darkness was setting in, so I made a hurried return to the warmth and relative comfort of the shack.

Seated on the air bed, I thought of home and Hy. My husband was probably working in his office at our house on Avila Street in San Francisco's Marina district. McCone & Ripinsky, our joint firm, had recently experienced an overload in his bailiwick—international security and executive protection. No wonder, given how crazy the world felt these days. Almost everybody was afraid and feeling vulnerable, although many weren't sure exactly what they feared.

I remembered accounts of the Cold War of the 1950s; at least then there'd been a recognizable adversary: the Russians, who had the bomb and were gaining the lead in the race to space. But now we were overwhelmed by threats from all sides: various violent factions in the Middle East; white power and other hate groups seemingly everywhere; crazies who wanted to use their bombs and guns against innocent schoolchildren; the Russians (again) interfering in our elections; unhinged people in our own government; mysterious viruses creeping around the world; even household products threatening to poison us all. Where and when would it all stop—if ever?

I smiled wryly. This was the kind of rant Hy would appreciate, but I hesitated to call him. It would only make me miss him more. Him and our cats, Alex and Jessie, who right now were probably making his life hell. They made their displeasure known when one or the other of us was away.

Well, enough woolgathering. I opened the iPad I'd brought with me—glad that I'd remembered my battery-powered charger—and pulled up the case file to add information on my day's progress.

Not much so far, at least in respect to the murders.

But Henry Howling Wolf's girlfriend, Sally Bee, had been missing for over forty-eight hours now. If the pendant was hers, how had she lost it? *Was* she another victim of the anonymous killer? Or was

MONDAY, JANUARY 7

10:00 a.m.

Allie Foxx had told me that the local tribal police had looked into the killings, but there was no copy of their report in the file the Sisters had provided. To my surprise, they had no office on the reservation. In Aspendale, however, I found that they had a small storefront in the middle of a side street. I introduced myself as Sharon McNear to its only occupant, a pleasant, stocky, middle-aged man named Herman Baldwing.

Baldwing looked like a cop, which he said he indeed had been for twenty years in Denver. "I was born on the rez here, but left to join the army when I was eighteen, then moved to Denver after my tour ended. But the city grew in ways I didn't like, so I ended up back here. It's a nice place—mostly."

I was interested in the "mostly."

Baldwing interrupted himself. "Where are my manners, as my ma used to ask? Please, sit down." He motioned at one of the chairs in front of his desk.

I sat.

"So you're interested in our dead girls?"

"Right. I came up here to write a travelogue, but I can't represent the area as a tourist destination until I have an idea of how the investigation is going."

He fiddled with a letter opener on his blotter. "The investigation is going exactly nowhere."

"Why?"

"Because the murders didn't happen on tribal land. We started to look into them and were told to butt out."

"By whom?"

"The county sheriff, Noah Arneson. He also told the FBI to butt out, and they did. Not their jurisdiction; nobody—that they know of—had crossed state lines."

"What about state authorities?"

"They respectfully declined. Their jurisdiction is over the highways. Neither girl was found by a highway. All we know is that we've lost two women in the prime years of their lives, and the authorities are stalling on finding out why."

"Is it possible to get a look at your files?"

He spread his big arms wide. "I might allow it, if I still had them. But I don't. They were confiscated."

"By whom?"

"The sheriff, who else?"

"How can he do that?"

"The problem here, as I've said, is with overlapping jurisdictions. Sheriff Arneson can do anything he wants within the county. We can do anything we want on the reservation. But there have been crimes that have been perpetrated by white men against Native women on the reservation, and when the men left the tribal lands they were immune from prosecution."

"That's unbelievable!"

He nodded. "And archaic, but until the lawmakers wake up and do something about it, our hands are tied."

"These lawmakers—"

"Are politicians. They don't want to offend their base. Look at how long it took to nominate a Black man for the state supreme court."

He was right about the whole scenario, but it made my blood boil. I controlled my anger and said, "If I have any other questions, may I call on you again?"

"Definitely. And good luck to you."

10:35 a.m.

After I left Baldwing's office, I debated going to the county seat to interview Sheriff Arneson and find out if he was as much of a horse's ass as Baldwing and Henry Howling Wolf had indicated, but I decided against it. From all indications he was aggressive and unpleasantly territorial. Given my present agitated state, a confrontation might result. And if my loosely constructed cover story didn't convince him, he'd probably make my life hell or sabotage my investigation in any way he could.

There was one man I could trust to give me facts about the county, so on the way into town I called Hal Bascomb, Hy's old friend who ran the airstrip. We hadn't had a chance to talk much when I flew in on Saturday, and now seemed like a good time if he was available.

It was another cold, mostly clear day—good flying

weather if there was no snow in the forecast—and Hal was at the airstrip. He said he'd be glad to come get me and that we could talk there. "The only traffic I've got is a student wobbling around, trying to figure out how to steer the trainer," he said.

"Are you sure it's safe to leave him?"

"Sure. If he steers into the ditch, he can learn how to pull it out."

10:55 a.m.

Hal picked me up in front of the Good Price Store, swung a U-turn, and headed back up the highway.

"Your student still wobbling?" I asked.

"Oh yeah. He shouldn't be wasting his money on lessons, 'cause he'll never make it as a pilot. Tries to steer with the yoke like you do a car, thinks the rudders are for braking. I tried to discourage him, but he's determined—and I need cash customers."

We arrived at the airstrip on the bluff above Aspendale, and soon we were seated inside the largest of the three Quonset huts in big old chairs by the wood stove. Hal provided coffee, looked out the door at the wobbler, and shook his head. He said, "So you want the dope on our little piece of heaven. Or hell, as the case may be."

"From a reliable source like you."

"Where should I start?"

"Anyplace."

"Okay. I'm not from here, you know. Grew up

in Oklahoma. Took up crop dusting there. Avoided a couple of wars, and then your hubby and I engaged in some...let's call them shenanigans...in Southeast Asia. After that I'd had enough of taking risks, so I looked around for someplace 'peaceful,' found out this strip was for sale, and here I am."

"You stressed the word 'peaceful.'"

"Yes, I did."

The UNICOM crackled and Hal spoke into it. "Okay, tie her down." He lowered the volume and said, "The Wobbler, asking permission to proceed to the tie-downs. Do you see any traffic out there? Does he need permission?"

I smiled, shook my head.

"Anyway," he went on, "we were talking about peaceful. *Not.* This is cowboy country. Bar-brawl country. I don't know how many times I've had to persuade drunks from taking off in their—or other people's—planes."

"How'd you persuade them?"

He grinned. "I used to be a golfer, and I still have a set of clubs."

"The sheriff ever interfere with what goes on up here?"

"Arneson? Hell no. He knows about my golf clubs and stays away."

"So what about other airstrips in the area?"

"Lots of them, but most are private—on ranches or big estates. The Harcourt place—or SupremeCourt, as they call it—is one example. Paved runway, lights, self-service fuel."

"Who are the Harcourts?"

"Rich ranchers, run cattle on a few thousand acres. I don't know them personally; they keep to themselves."

"How many of them are there?"

"Three. The father, Ben Harcourt—known in these parts as the Old Man—is a widower; his wife died years ago. The sons, Paul and Kurt, are in their thirties or forties."

The "Old Man" must be the one Gene and Vic worked for.

"Do you know anything about their employees? Particularly a pair of men named Gene and Vic?"

He paused. "I'm not personally acquainted with either of them, but I know thugs when I see some."

"What do they do at the ranch?"

"Beats me. Mainly when I see them, it's in town."

"They ever show up here?"

"Nope. Like I said, that bunch keeps to themselves, and that includes the employees. Sorry I can't tell you more. When I said I came up here for peace and quiet, I meant it."

Hal and I had another cup of coffee and did some catching up on his, Hy's, and my varied activities. He'd turned into a glider enthusiast and offered to take me up. I said maybe, but meant no. I don't mind the capricious winds that buffet airplanes, but I don't trust updrafts and downdrafts when I don't have an engine to rely on.

12:28 p.m.

Back in Aspendale, I walked along the main street, looking for someone else to talk with. There was a lumberyard, a fairly large one, at the eastern edge of town, and near the front gate, two men were lifting sheets of plywood onto a flatbed truck. I wandered down there, stopped close by to watch them.

It didn't take long for both men to notice me. The closest looked longest, but I couldn't tell if he was staring at my face or the pendant around my neck.

I said, "When you're done there, maybe one of you could help me."

The one who'd stared at me paused in his loading. "Help you how?" According to a logo on the shirt he wore, he was an employee of the lumberyard. He was the younger of the two, with a tanned face marred by a jagged scar above his right eyebrow and thick black hair down to his shoulders. The other, perhaps in his late forties, was bald, with a fringe of red hair, a flushed face, and an enormous belly.

"I'm interested in what grades of lumber you carry, and what has to be special-ordered."

"Sure. This won't take long."

When he finished and came out to talk, he gave me the usual male once-over and seemed to like what he saw. "So, what are you thinking of doing with this lumber?" he asked.

"I've been toying with having a cabin built in the area."

"Oh, where?"

"I haven't gotten that far yet. I'm a travel writer,

doing a piece on the county, and the idea of a getaway cabin has always interested me. I'm at a motel right now, and it isn't too great."

"Which one?"

"The E-Z Rest."

He made a face. "A dump."

"It is, but for now it's all right."

"Where is it you want to get away from?"

"The Bay Area."

"Well, I don't blame you. As for lumber, we carry the standard varieties—pine, oak, redwood. You want anything exotic like mahogany, we can order it."

I laughed, returning his appreciative look with one of my own. "I don't think mahogany would fit in with a rustic cabin motif—or my budget."

"You have an architect?"

"What I'm thinking of doesn't require an architect."

"You'll need a real estate agent, though. I can recommend—"

"Maybe on my next trip here. Right now I've got to familiarize myself with the area and write my article."

"I gotcha."

To prolong the conversation, I said, "I was also wondering about snow tires for my car. There's already been some snow, and I wonder what kind you'd recommend I buy?"

"That would depend on what kind of car you have, how far you want to drive, and other factors."

"I see. I don't have it here with me, but I'll have a Jeep pretty soon."

"A good vehicle for these parts." His gaze lowered. "That's a nice pendant you're wearing."

"Thanks, Mr.—"

"Blue. Jake Blue." One of the hunters who had found the bodies. "And your name is?"

"Sharon McNear."

"Well, Sharon, how about I buy you a beer at the Brews? Say about four?"

"At the...Oh, the bar over there." I motioned toward the nearby building.

"Yeah. A good way to wind down the day."

"That sounds fine."

As I walked away, I wondered about Jake Blue's re-action to the pendant. Had he recognized it? Known who the owner was? Or that Henry Howling Wolf had made it? Was his interest in me only the reaction of a man to a new woman in town, or something else? Well, one way or another, I'd find out this afternoon.

2:21 p.m.

After a late lunch I made a few purchases in the hard-ware store that would make me feel more secure in the shack: a sturdy length of chain, two new padlocks, a heavy-duty hasp, and the tools to install them. The man who rang me up was as uncommunicative as the one in the food store. I assumed it was because they didn't care for Native women.

4:01 p.m.

Billiards 'n Brews, aka the Brews, was housed in a
long corrugated iron building that might once have
been a warehouse. Inside it was dimly lit and hollowly
echoed the sounds of two men playing dice at the
bar. Two pool tables sat unused. Booths lined the side
walls, and in one of them Jake Blue sat, a pitcher of
beer and two glasses in front of him.

"You're a minute late," he said, smiling. "I hate to be
separated from my first beer of the day that long."

"Pour! Drink!" I smiled back and sat down across
from him.

We drank. His eyes left mine; this time I knew he
was looking at the pendant. Abruptly he said, "I have
to ask you about that pendant you're wearing."

"Yes?"

"Where'd you get it? It doesn't look new."

"Found it."

"Oh? Where?"

"On one of my walks in the woods."

"My sister, Josie, had one like it. It's pretty rare."

"Henry Howling Wolf told me he only made three,
one for a woman who died. Would that be your
sister?"

"Yes."

"I'm sorry, Jake."

"So am I." His voice was bitter. "Josie loved her
pendant, hardly ever took it off. It was buried with
her. Who did this one belong to?"

"I don't know." I didn't add that it probably belonged to Henry's girlfriend, Sally Bee.

Jake took another swallow of beer. "So what did you do after you left the lumberyard?" he asked.

"Wandered."

"Now that would be the life—wandering."

"I don't have anything better to do. I'm just waiting...well, maybe for an insight."

"Huh?"

"Into which way my article's going to go. I was told something today that makes me wonder if I've come to the wrong place."

"Oh? What?"

"About Native women being killed around here."

"Yeah. That." He expelled his breath harshly, took a long drink of beer.

"The person who told me didn't offer any details. Would you mind telling me about it?"

"I guess not, if you want me to. So happens I found them."

"Oh no!"

"Yeah. The way it went, my buddy Bart Upstream and I were out hunting. Pheasant season. There's an old monastery that's a good place for birds. So we were moving along, real quiet like, and I practically stumbled over Sam Runs Close on the ground with a bullet hole in her forehead."

"Runs Close? Who was she?"

"Good kid. Kind of strident when she got her back up about Indigenous women's rights, but her heart was in the right place." He finished his beer, poured more into his glass. "Then Bart yells, and there's Dierdra Two Shoes, dead too."

"Must've been awful for you."

"Christ, yes, but seeing Dierdra was worse on Bart.

They'd been involved pretty heavy a couple of years ago. Of course, that was over quick enough when she started going out on him."

"Going out? With whom?"

"Don't know. All of a sudden, little Dierdra wasn't available any more. Who told you about the murders, anyway?"

"Somebody in one of the stores. A tourist, I think, who was kind of freaked out by it."

"Well, it's damn freaky, all right."

"Do you have any idea who committed the murders? Or why?"

"It's got to be somebody who hates Natives, hates women. Maybe..." Jake paused, anger coloring his face. "Maybe one of the Harcourts."

"Who're they?"

"Big cattle ranchers, own a forty-five-thousand-acre spread out past the buttes."

I made an effort to underplay my interest. "I've noticed there are a lot of ranches in the area."

"Not so many as there used to be."

"How come?"

"Ben Harcourt has been buying out the others. It's like he wants to own all the grazing land."

"He's not somebody new in the area, is he?"

"Nope. One of the old-timers."

"An old man?"

He laughed without humor. "Ben's not that old—he's probably no more than sixty. But everybody calls him the Old Man."

"What's he like?"

"Autocratic. Acts like he's trying to establish a dynasty. You'd think he'd have more sense, given the quality of his sons. Well, Kurt's not so bad, but I don't think his interests are in cattle. He's got an education from some eastern college, used to teach at USC. Chemistry, or something like that."

"Why'd he come back here?"

Jake rubbed his fingers together. "Money, baby. Daddy called, and Kurt said, 'Yessir.' Now, his brother Paul is a piece of work. Or maybe I shouldn't link the word 'work' to him. Lazy son of a bitch, hangs out all day at the Back Woods Casino. Most nights, the whole damn family's there."

"I gather you don't like them."

"Not one bit. Assholes, all three of them."

"What about the guys who work for them—Gene and Vic? I ran into them at the Good Price Store and they offered to buy me a beer."

"Gene Byram and Vic Long. Yeah, the same applies. You should stay away from them. They're bad news."

"I'll keep a wide berth. Is the Back Woods a Native casino?"

"No. It's an illegal operation, owned by some of the powerful white interests around here. Probably that's why they hang there; they hate Natives. According to the Old Man, our people are the worst thing that ever happened to America."

"He doesn't have too much of a grasp of history, does he?"

"Nope."

"Where is this casino?"

"You planning on going there?"

"Maybe. I'd like to get a look at the Harcourts."

"Why?"

"Well, they're prominent citizens in the area. I might want to mention them in my article."

"The Harcourts are against any sort of publicity. Besides, you'd stand out at the casino."

"Why?"

"You're Native, aren't you?"

"Yes—Shoshone. But I was raised by a white family, who claimed I was a 'throwback' to a Native ancestor. I only found out about my roots in my thirties."

"That must've been a shock."

"It was, but after I'd tracked down my birth parents, I suspected I'd known all along that something wasn't right. And now I have two families and love them both."

"Well, Natives aren't welcome there, women or men." He studied my face. "Of course, if you were raised white, you've got the right mannerisms. They'll put up with Natives if they clean up nice."

"I clean up nice, when I want to."

"Maybe you'll get by, then. The casino isn't all that fancy."

"Do you go there?"

"Hell, no. I avoid the place like the plague." He took a fresh napkin from the holder and drew me a map through the surrounding forest. "It's about a fifteen- or twenty-minute walk. You need me for anything, I'll be right here, probably in this same booth. In fact, why don't you meet me at around eleven, let me know what you found out."

"Okay. See you then."

8:21 p.m.

I selected a pair of black jeans and a red silk blouse from the limited wardrobe I'd brought along and coiled my hair into a knot on top of my head. I put on my own parka, which was in far better shape than the Sisters', a wool cap, and gloves. Before leaving the shack, I placed the plastic packet containing my identification and .38 in an inside pocket.

Following the directions I'd gotten from Jake Blue, I set out through the forest, my flashlight showing the way. The night was bitter cold, and there were patches of ice that I was extra careful to avoid. I hoped it wouldn't snow again before I got back.

I wasn't planning to gamble at the casino. Fortunately, gambling is one of the vices left out of my makeup. But I would attempt to connect with the Harcourt family if they were there.

The casino was housed in a big geodesic dome with several smaller ones attached. I'd seen its garish flashing lights reflected on the trees from at least half a mile away. Music filled the surrounding forest—a monotonous rock beat. Cars and trucks were parked helter-skelter in the dirt lot, and a few people huddled together outside, smoking or indulging in whatever was their pleasure.

There was a doorman at the entrance to the big dome who looked at me skeptically but made no attempt to stop me from entering. Inside, a pair of blond, fur-coated women shied away from me as if I had a communicable disease. The place was crowded with similar white types. They acted as if I smelled bad.

Actually it was the casino itself that smelled bad; it reeked of smoke, both tobacco and marijuana. Smoking in public establishments is illegal in California, but then so is gambling, except on the reservations. That hadn't stopped them here.

Tables—blackjack, poker, roulette—crowded the dome, and there were banks of slot machines. Waitresses in scanty red outfits and preposterously high heels served drinks to the players and kibitzers. Chips clattered, bells bonged, shouts went up from the tables. Women in workers' gloves pulled tirelessly at the handles of slots. Dim lighting gave permission for people to perform acts that they never would have in the privacy of their own homes: men fingered cocktail waitresses' asses; women cozied up to much younger men; drinks spilled, bettors staggered, arguments erupted. And yet there was a kind of innocence about all this frantic activity: they were greedy children on the playground before the final bell rang.

As I stood looking around, a young brown-haired man in a security guard's uniform approached me. "Ms. McNear?" he asked.

"Yes?" I said warily.

"I'm Tom Williams, a friend of Jake Blue. He called and told me you'd be in. Said you were interested in the Harcourts."

I smiled and shook his hand, concealing my annoyance at Jake's interference. Did he think I needed help in finding the Harcourts? Or was he checking up on me for some reason?

Williams and I walked through the main room,

which also contained two cocktail lounges and a large snack bar. As we went, I was on the receiving end of a few dark looks that reminded me yet again of the prevailing attitude toward Natives. A man in a denim jacket started to jostle me, then turned away when he saw I was with Williams.

The reactions surprised me. I had seldom been the target of blatant racism before. I'd been raised in a section of San Diego where white, Hispanic, Black, and various other races lived in relative harmony. In college at UC Berkeley being a person of color was considered a plus. And San Francisco was much the same. Here, however, my eyes were being opened to all sorts of negative behaviors.

"This is where the action is," Tom said. "See that blond gent over there at the craps table? That's Paul Harcourt, tonight's big winner."

An impressive pile of chips sat in front of Harcourt, and a small crowd of onlookers were cheering him on. He was tall, well over six feet, and handsome, with a trim, athletic body clothed in what reminded me of a 1970s leisure suit. He laughed a lot with his audience, his blue eyes crinkling at their corners, his ultra-white teeth flashing. He raked in chips and laughed some more, and when he cashed out, he left a generous tip for the croupier.

"Aren't his family major stakeholders in the casino?" I asked Tom.

"Sure, they practically live here. He'll join the rest of the family in the cocktail lounge."

"I'd like to meet them."

"I'm not sure they'll welcome a journalist, but I'll introduce you."

In the lounge, Paul Harcourt sat down in a booth with a silver-haired older man and another blond man who looked enough like him to be his twin. Tom and I loitered near the entrance as the waitress delivered them draft beers.

"The Old Man," Tom said, "is supposedly very ill—kidney trouble, arrhythmia, bladder problems. But that could change; I hear that he's going to start having some experimental treatments pretty soon."

"Oh? What kind?"

"Don't know." He steered me closer.

Paul Harcourt's eyes focused on me, narrowed. He elbowed the white-haired man next to him, and they both stared. Then the other man shrugged and looked away. Still staring at me, Paul started to get up, then changed his mind and stayed put.

Tom said, "Hi, folks. This is Sharon McNear, a journalist who's here to do a travel piece on the county."

The Harcourts exchanged looks. The Old Man shook his head. Paul said, "We don't encourage publicity."

I said, "Not even in the interests of improving tourism in this area?"

"We get plenty of tourists in season."

The other blond, who I assumed was his brother, Kurt, added, "You can't judge a place by what it's like in January."

"But I can extrapolate what it's like at the height of the summer season."

"I'm not so sure there is such a thing as the summer season here."

Tom gave me a look that said, "You're on your own," and moved away from me.

"Meruk County's been unfairly ignored by the press," I said to the Old Man. "I understand your family owns a large cattle ranch, Mr. Harcourt, which is why I wanted to meet you. Ranching is a primary business here, isn't it?"

"That's right. It's our lifeblood."

"I also understand you have a large airstrip. I imagine it's necessary to patrol your land from a plane."

He nodded. Kurt said, "Patrolling by air is standard procedure on a ranch as large as ours. Cattle...well, frankly, they're not very well endowed with brains or good sense. They wander off, get in trouble, and then it's up to us to rescue them. We pinpoint the location and then send the ranch hands out."

"Do all three of you fly, Mr. Harcourt?"

Ben Harcourt said sharply, "You don't intend to write about us, do you?"

"Well, I hear you're very prominent citizens."

"We value our privacy, miss."

"So we'd rather you didn't use our names in your article," Paul added with a scowl.

Kurt's manner was less hostile. "If you want to mention cattle ranching, I can put you in touch with some knowledgeable people in the county agriculture department."

"All right. Thank you."

Then the Old Man drained his drink and said to his sons, ignoring me, "It's getting late. If you boys don't mind, I'll ask Andy to drive me home now."

"Sure, Dad." They spoke in unison and stood up.

Paul helped him from the booth. The Old Man tried to protest but gave in as his son guided him out into the lobby.

Kurt said, "I need to be going too. Thanks for your interest, Ms. McNear."

"Wait. The story will run in the *San Francisco Chronicle* and the *Sacramento Bee*. The *L.A. Times* too, although we haven't firmed up our agreement yet. That's excellent coverage." Fortunately I had friends and acquaintances at many newspapers who would back up any inquiries.

"I'm sorry. As my father said, we have no interest in publicity."

I watched as he joined his brother and they went outside.

10:05 p.m.

Jake Blue was sitting in the same booth as before, staring into a half-full beer stein when I arrived at Billiards 'n Brews. The place was doing a fair amount of business, the jukebox playing retro rock, but nobody was dancing. The patrons slouched in their chairs, some chatting with their companions but most not. A curiously subdued scene.

Jake ordered a beer for me. Then he said, "You have a good time at the casino?"

"I wouldn't call it that, but your friend Tom put me in touch with the Harcourts. Thanks to you."

"I hope you don't mind my asking him to help you out."

"Depends on why you did."

"Just wanted to make sure you were okay. That casino can be a pretty rough place for a Native. What did you think of the Harcourt bunch?"

"I couldn't get a good read on them. They're unusually shy of publicity."

"They should be. The Old Man used to mix it up pretty much—bar brawls, started wrecking cars back in the nineties."

"Drunk driving?"

"Oh yeah. Drunk and entitled—bad combination. Both of the boys there too?"

"Yes, but they're hardly boys."

"They are to me. Two cases of arrested development. Overprivileged, overeducated bastards with more money than good sense."

"They really make you angry. Why?"

For a few seconds he stared down at his beer glass, and his fingers tightened on it. He took a deep swallow, expelled his breath slowly.

Finally he said, "My sister, Josie, was killed four years ago. I think one of them might have done it."

10:27 p.m.

Over our drinks, Jake told me about his sister's murder. Josie had gotten her degree in education from UC Berkeley and returned to teach on the elementary level in the Meruk schools. Four years ago, her body had been found in the woods a mile or so from where the two other Indigenous women later died; she'd been roughed up and strangled. No one had ever been arrested for the crime.

Could her murder be related to the recent murders? It seemed unlikely because of the four-year time difference and the fact that the methods were not the same. Still, it was possible that there was some sort of connection.

"I still don't understand why you think one of the Harcourts was responsible," I said. "Were they friends of Josie's? Did she date one of the sons? Did she owe them money?"

"She didn't believe in borrowing money. She may have dated one of the sons, I'm not sure. She was seen with either Paul or Kurt shortly before she died."

"With *either* Paul or Kurt?"

"The person who saw them wasn't sure. It was from a distance and they look a lot alike."

"Josie didn't say anything to you about it?"

"No. When we were growing up together, she was open, confided in me, but after she came back from Berkeley, all that had changed. She was very private. No, more than private—secretive."

"Were you able to get a look at the sheriff's department's files of their investigation?"

He laughed bitterly. "They didn't want to release them to me, even though I was her next of kin. They gave in when I mentioned the Freedom of Information Act. Stupid bastards didn't know that it only applies on the federal level."

"Did you keep the copies?"

"Sure I did."

"May I see them?"

"Why? You're not going to write about Josie's murder?"

"No. Call it journalistic curiosity. But I am going to mention the murders of the Native women."

"What for?"

I decided to go with the most believable explanation. "I'm Native myself and I have a vested interest."

He was silent for a time, glowering into his glass. Then he said, "All right, you can see the files. But I want them back."

"Of course."

"I could bring them to you at the E-Z Rest."

"I'd prefer to pick them up at your place."

He frowned, then shrugged. I could tell that talking of his sister's murder had taken a lot out of him; all the flirtatiousness he'd displayed when we first met was gone. "All right," he said listlessly. He signed a tab that lay on the table, and we left the Brews.

It was a short walk to a side street where he entered a small, brown-shingled cottage and returned with a thin folder. I tucked it into the pocket of my parka and headed back to the shack.

11:47 p.m.

I was shivering by the time I reached the shack. A thick layer of clouds covered the sky, making the night inky black, and with the windchill the temperature must have been close to zero.

The shack was frosty white in the beam from my flashlight as I stepped up to the door. I couldn't wait to get inside and warm up. I switched the light to my left hand, got the padlock key out of my pocket, and started to insert it.

Scraping sounds behind me.

I tensed, turned in time to see a shadowy form with an upraised arm but not in time to duck out of the way. A glancing blow landed on my arm, jarring the flashlight loose, then strong hands shoved me to the ground.

The light went out when the flash landed on the muddy ground. Stunned, I lay prone in the darkness. The hands pawed at my upper body, then my neck, as if the attacker intended to strangle me. I sucked in my breath, my throat and lungs burning from the cold, and lashed out with my legs, connecting solidly with some part of the attacker. He—yes, definitely a male—yelped and his hands jerked off me. I drew back to kick again, but he'd had enough. I heard his footsteps running away down the slope.

Had the son of a bitch been trying to kill me? There didn't seem to be any other reason for the attack. He hadn't made any effort to get at the folder or the pouch containing my identification and the .38 in the inner safety pocket of the parka.

I lifted onto my hands and knees. When I turned my head, wincing, I saw the beam of his flashlight come on, pointed away from me, making erratic splashes of light in the darkness as he ran. Seconds later I heard him splash through the water under the stone bridge, and he and the light disappeared into the woods.

Still groggy, I groped for the flashlight. Luckily it hadn't broken; the beam came on when I shook it and flicked the switch. I'd dropped my keys too, but I was able to find them with the light. I got to my feet and leaned against the door while I fumbled the key into the padlock and got it open.

Inside I lit the lanterns and took one of them into the bathroom to inspect the damage in the mirror. There was a small bump on my head and a little blood where the skin had been broken, and a thin red scratch around my neck. I fingered it, wincing.

And then I realized that the silver pendant was gone.

The attacker *hadn't* tried to strangle me; it was the pendant he'd been after. Who? Jake? Henry Howling Wolf? I couldn't imagine why either of them, or anybody else who'd seen me wearing it, would want it badly enough to assault me to get it.

Had he followed me here from Aspendale? I'd been alert when I left the village and on the walk through the woods, as always, and hadn't seen or heard anyone. Or had he somehow found out I was staying here and lain in wait for me?

My head ached and my vision was slightly blurred. I didn't think I was badly hurt, but my body cried out for rest. I got into the bunk and used an old breathing trick to relax so I could sleep.

TUESDAY, JANUARY 8

I still had a headache when I woke up, but it was muted and tolerable. I ate a light breakfast, even though I wasn't hungry, and that helped ease the pain and let me concentrate on the sheriff's department files Jake had given me.

The files were sketchy, proving out my theory that Indigenous women—even murdered Indigenous women—weren't high on the government's list of priorities. Josie Blue had become a teacher at the Meruk Unified Elementary School, popular with the students because she shared their roots and understood their problems. Then, just short of four years ago—a year after her brother told me she'd become remote and unsettled—her body had been found by a hiker in the woods near St. Germaine.

Josie's time away at UC Berkeley had changed her. The woman who returned to Meruk County was not the woman who had left. While not truly sophisticated, she'd become polished: nearly six feet tall, she was thin, with straight hair falling to her waist; her clothing had a bohemian touch, and most of her ensembles were her own creations. Many of the local men were interested in her, but when she didn't reciprocate, the inevitable rumors began to spread: she had a secret lover who was probably married, she was a lesbian, she was just plain stupid for not appreciating them, she was allied with some strange Berkeley-type cult.

Some men will blame a woman for anything rather than themselves if they can't get a date.

When Josie's body was found, there was an outcry from the more liberal citizens of the area, but no suspects were interrogated. And there was no mention of any of the Harcourts.

I understood Jake Blue's frustration. The files raised more questions than they answered.

11:00 a.m.

After I finished with the files, I put them back in the folder and went into Aspendale to return them to Jake. As I walked toward the lumberyard I passed several people on the streets. Most walked quickly with their heads down, not acknowledging me or anyone else. Odd behavior for residents of a place where everybody must know everybody else. Even though it was a beautiful day, an atmosphere of gloom that I hadn't noticed the day before seemed to have settled over the town. Maybe the residents were just having a collective bad Tuesday.

When I reached the lumberyard I found Jake on a coffee break, leaning against one of the trucks at the loading dock and talking with its driver. When he saw me, he came over and gave me a long, searching look as I handed him the folder.

"Nothing much in them, is there?" he said.

"Aside from the information on your sister, no."

"I'd rather not talk any more about Josie. I've got something to tell you."

"Yes?"

"I went back to the Brews after you left last night and Bart Upstream was there. I told him about your interest in the murders and he said he'd talk, maybe bring Fowler Runs Close with him."

"Fowler Runs Close?"

"The dead woman's younger brother. He and Bart work construction together. Can you be at my house at three this afternoon?"

"Sure. Thanks for setting it up."

"No problem. Bart has a key. He and Fowler should be there waiting when you get there."

3:00 p.m.

They weren't at the cottage when I arrived. I sat on the porch for ten minutes before they showed up in a Ford Bronco. Bart introduced himself and Fowler Runs Close, then unlocked the door and ushered me into a comfortable room where shabby, overstuffed furnishings centered on a native stone fireplace.

Bart Upstream was a handsome man in his early twenties, with strong cheekbones, large amber eyes, and a silky ponytail that fell below his clavicle. Fowler was in his late teens, short, and walked with a hunched gait, hands thrust into the pockets of his brown faux leather jacket. As he sat down he rubbed self-consciously at a rash on his left cheek.

I opened the conversation by thanking them for talking to me.

"Don't thank me," Fowler said. "Damn journalist trying to make money off of our grief. Why do you think my sister's murder is any of your business?"

"For one thing, I'm not going to make much money, if any. Freelance journalists aren't well paid. And second, it's natural I'd be interested, being Native myself. The local law doesn't seem much concerned."

"Fuckin' white pigs! Wouldn't be surprised if the scumbag was one of them."

"Cool it, man," Bart said.

Fowler ignored him. "You're supposed to be skin like us," he said to me. "What're you doin' sidin' with those white pigs?"

"I'm not siding with them. Just the opposite. You may be right that somebody in law enforcement is covering up, if nothing else. Bad seeds can turn up in almost every police agency."

"Yeah, like that asshole Arneson."

"Do you really think he had something to do with the murders?"

"How the hell should I know? If I find out he did, he's dead meat."

"Cool it, Fowler!" Bart half rose from his seat.

"Shit!" Fowler stood and pushed past him. "I got no time for this."

He stalked out and slammed the door behind him.

"He's upset about Sam...about everything," Bart said. "And about all of a sudden having the responsibility for their pa being dumped in his lap. Sam was so capable, she took care of both of them and the house and worked too. Fowler can't measure up to that. He can't cook or clean, and he's never held a job more than a month at a time."

"Anybody can learn to cook and clean and hold a job."

"Yeah, I know. Sam spoiled him."

"Or maybe she just did everything because it was easier."

"Not Sam. She never did anything the easy way. She was kind of a free spirit. Did what she did when she wanted to, and the hell with what anybody else thought. Her father abandoned the family—familiar story around here—when she was maybe ten. Her mother died of tuberculosis—another familiar story—about five years later. In addition to Fowler, Sam had a younger brother Bobby, and she tried to take care of him, but he hooked up with one of the gangs and got stabbed to death during a fight. After that she went wild: booze, men, outrageous behavior. Everybody but her closest friends abandoned her, but finally she turned around and put her energy into Indigenous causes."

"You were one of those friends who didn't abandon her," I said.

"Yeah, I was. And that's why these murders are tearing me up. She had so much to give. So did Dierdra, in her way."

"If you don't mind, let's talk about you and Dierdra."

He was silent.

"Jake said the two of you might've gotten married."

"Might've. I was thinking we could get away from here, move over to Reno. I worked in a casino there for a while; I'd already called them and they said they'd be glad to hire me back. Dierdra, she had experience waitressing in the café; she could've gotten on someplace too. We could've made it. But then she decided she didn't want to be tied down and started running around with other guys. We had a big fight about it the night before she—" He shook his head, clamped the palm of his right hand over his eyes.

I waited until he got control of himself. "Do you have any idea who might have wanted her dead? One of the other guys she was running around with?"

"Maybe. Her mother might know who they were, but I don't." He paused, frowning. "Fowler mentioned Arneson before. For all we know he's the one going around whacking Native women—maybe thinks it's his civic duty."

"What about those cattle ranchers, the Harcourts?"

Bart looked thoughtful. "I don't see what they'd have to gain by killing."

"Kicks?"

"Nah. Those are serious people. You should've seen the Old Man when he came into town a couple of years ago: he looked like the guy in that picture of the farmer with his wife and the pitchfork."

I'd seen *American Gothic* once at the Art Institute of Chicago, and I had to agree the comparison was apt.

"Not that he comes in much any more," Bart added. "I hear he's pretty sick. And they've got an airstrip, have a lot of supplies flown in. It's a pretty fancy one, a guy I know who flies told me. Paved, with lots of lights, not a grass strip like most of the others around here. Guess they figure grass is for cattle."

He tried to smile at his feeble joke, but his lips trembled and the smile fell apart. He looked at his watch. "Gotta get back on the job."

I stood when he did. "If you think of anything about Sam's last days that might—however unimportant—have to do with her murder, will you let me know?"

"Sure. Where can I find you?"

"Tell Jake. I'll keep in touch with him."

3:41 p.m.

Jake had suggested I wait at his cottage until he got home from work. It seemed a waste of time. I thought again about going to the sheriff's headquarters and trying to speak with Noah Arneson, but that would mean borrowing a car for the thirty-minute drive, and there was no guarantee that he'd even be there. Besides, I'd need a good excuse to see him, and then I'd have to be very careful not to say anything that would blow my cover. And I wasn't about to schedule an appointment either; throughout my career I've found that just showing up works best with unwilling and potentially hostile subjects.

After half an hour I yielded to impulse and began snooping through the house—after all, there was no guarantee that Jake Blue wasn't the man who'd attacked me last night, or the perpetrator of the two murders. He had given me no reason to suspect him, but for all I knew he could have withheld something or other that had relevance to my investigation. I couldn't afford to trust any of these strangers.

I started with the bedroom, where secrets are often found. The bed was neatly made, the socks, T-shirts, and underwear in the bureau drawers aligned precisely. The single nightstand held tissues, nail clippers, aspirin, and a mild analgesic for muscle pain. The closet contained work clothes, a few ties, and a single suit whose extra-narrow lapels were several years out of date. There was nothing unusual in the adjoining bathroom and medicine chest.

The kitchen: a fifties-style range showing signs of use, but scrubbed clean; a fridge of the same vintage containing eggs, milk, beer, orange juice, carrots, and a badly wilted bunch of kale; its tiny freezer compartment held a few boxes of Stouffer's macaroni and cheese. The cabinets were full of mismatched dishes, bowls, and pots and pans, the drawers a jumble of equally mismatched utensils. Jake, I thought, had no claim to culinary expertise.

I stood in the middle of the room, my eyes narrowed as I took a final look around. Kitchens had been the source of some of my better finds in the past. Including refrigerators. I opened the freezer compartment again, removed the mac and cheese. The crusted ice was thick. I scraped at it here and there, and one of my fingernails hit what felt like glass. I got a soft spatula from one of the jumbled drawers and moved it carefully over the spot. A narrow unlabeled vial, perhaps three inches in length, came into view. I worked with the spatula until I could remove it.

A cloudy substance. What the hell was it? And why had Jake Blue hidden a vial of it in his freezer?

I put the vial in my pocket and returned to the living room—and in good time too, because shortly after five, Jake came through the door. "Ah, good, you're still here. I'll get us drinks!"

He went through the door to the kitchen, and I heard the whirring of a wine opener. When he returned he had a bottle of Sangiovese and two glasses. "This is from a winery down in the hills in Mendocino County. Friend of mine works there, gets me a deep discount."

Together we sipped in silence, neither of us anxious to discuss the issues of the day. The wine was excellent.

There's a myth about Native people: they can't drink alcohol without becoming crazed drunks. Not so. The "genetic theory" of Native Americans' intolerance to alcohol has largely been refuted, but it still is accepted by many people because of unscientific motivations—one of them being bigotry. In truth, the Natives had no alcohol until they were introduced to it by Europeans, in an attempt to influence them to give up treaty rights. High alcohol use can be attributed to helplessness, poverty, and a bad lifestyle— none of which the Natives have cornered the market on. Yes, some Natives get drunk and raise hell—as do people who are Black, white, Asian, and possibly extraterrestrial.

I myself have gotten drunk and raised hell, but I've never been accused of my behavior being caused by genetics. Jeez, I was just having a good time!

We discussed my meeting with Bart and Fowler. Jake gave an exasperated sigh. "Fowler's always been a shithead. I'm surprised that Sam didn't cut him loose years ago. But that was Sam—too big a heart for her own good."

"She must've had a lot of patience too."

"More than Fowler deserved. I wonder what's going to happen to him now."

"There's no other family he can turn to?"

"Maybe on the rez. But Fowler, like a lot of his generation, doesn't want to be seen as Native. And he certainly doesn't want to live hardscrabble, like they do out there. For that, I don't blame him."

We drifted off into other topics. I probed a little further about his sister Josie's murder, but today he didn't seem to want to discuss it, so I let the subject lapse. An hour later, I told him I had to go. He offered to walk me to where I was staying, and I declined.

6:10 p.m.

Seated on a bench outside an eatery called the Owl Cafe, I put in a call to M&R in San Francisco. Ted Smalley, the agency's office manager, answered and immediately said, "We've been wondering when you'd check in. How are you? Any progress?"

"Some. Nothing definite to report as yet."

"Who do you want to talk with?"

"Hy and Mick. And you."

He sighed and said grumpily, "So I come in last. An afterthought."

"You sound like you're in a snit."

"Just lost an auction on eBay."

"For what?"

"A terrific Botany 500 sport coat. Black Watch plaid with hand-applied glitter strips. I'm in mourning."

Ted has been making what he calls "fashion statements" for most of his adult life. They've ranged from grunge to Hawaiian to cowboy to Edwardian, but the most lasting has been Botany 500, a long-defunct producer of sartorial atrocities.

"Oh, that's too bad."

"You're being insincere. I'm thinking of going back to grunge."

The first time I'd met Ted, when he was the receptionist at All Souls Legal Cooperative in San Francisco's Bernal Heights district, he'd been deeply into grunge. All I could see of him at first was his big, bare feet propped on the desk, and only his winning smile as he peered over them kept me from fleeing my interview for the job of staff investigator.

"What does Neal think of you going back to grunge?" I asked. Neal Osborn, his husband, dresses like an English barrister.

"Not much, I guess. Although he suggested I consider wearing caftans."

"Why not? There are a lot of beautiful ones available."

"No way. They're too long, and I trip a lot as is."

"Uh-huh. Is Hy in his office?"

"No, he left a while ago, said he was heading for L.A.—some CEO getting nervous about his so-called enemies."

I was disappointed, but not surprised. Hy is a top-flight hostage negotiator, but many of his jobs in executive protection are simply exercises in hand-holding.

"What about Mick?"

"He's here. I'll buzz him."

My nephew came on the line quickly. "Shar! I was wondering when we'd hear from you. Are you calling on your cell? The connection's kind of staticky."

"No. One of the clients gave me a phone with a local provider. Mine doesn't work up here." I gave him the number, then said, "Listen, I have a vial of some liquid I need analyzed. There's a pilot up here whom I think I can bribe to fly it down to you. You still have your lab contact?"

"Of course. Just tell the pilot to notify me about when he's arriving. Oakland, right?"

"Yes." The landing fees at SFO were outrageous. "Also," I went on, "I need information about a number of people. You ready?" I read off a list: the two murdered women, the Harcourts, Gene Byram and Vic Long, Henry Howling Wolf, Sally Bee, Jake Blue, and his sister, Josie.

Mick said, "I suppose you want this tomorrow morning?"

"ASAP."

"Well, Derek and I are at loose ends these days, so he can help." Derek Frye was his counterpart at the agency as well as a partner in several outside computer services ventures.

"Why at loose ends?"

"No prospects. No possibilities. I don't know what's wrong with the women in this town."

"Maybe they're all wondering what's wrong with *you.*"

"Shar . . . Okay, I'll get back to you. But how can I?"

"I'll get back to *you.*"

As I disconnected, I also wondered what *was* wrong with the young straight women of San Francisco. Mick and Derek were stars of the tech world, having built and sold two innovative sites that had made them millions. Yet he and Derek—in spite of being good-looking, personable men—were dateless most nights these days, easily available for my many requests to which any ordinary employee would've said, "Stuff it."

A good deal for me, since that meant I could tap into their expertise at almost any time, and I was grateful for their willingness to help out at a moment's notice. I didn't know much about Derek's private life, but Mick had been through several disappointments in his relationships that had left him scorched and extremely wary of becoming involved again.

I called Hal Bascomb at the airstrip, explained that I needed a package delivered to Oakland.

"No problem," he said. "I've got a chichi couple who want me to take them to SFO so they can catch their flight to Argentina. I can put the package in your nephew's hands by midnight. Give me a number where I can reach him."

I did, then asked, "How can I get the package to you?"

"I'll come get it. Where are you?"

I told him.

"See you in fifteen minutes."

"Thanks, Hal."

I wondered why Hy was on his way to L.A. and considered trying to call him while I waited. No, no point in it. When he was in transit, he almost always switched his cell to voice mail.

Hal arrived. I'd wrapped the vial in several plastic freezer bags also appropriated from Jake's kitchen. After turning the parcel over to him, I headed back through the forest to the shack, making my way slowly and warily over the ice-slick ground. I held the flashlight in my left hand, my right hand on the .38 in the parka's outside pocket. I wasn't taking any chances on being caught unawares after what had happened last night.

No one had been at the shack since I'd left it; the new chain and lock hadn't been touched. I went inside, made myself a sandwich, and settled down to read some more of the tattered paperback of *War and Peace* that I'd brought along.

I've actually read the entire book—including the battle scenes, but now I take it with me whenever I have to travel, hoping that one day I'll understand it. Or at least understand why Leo Tolstoy had wanted to gift the world with a mostly boring novel of over a thousand pages. It's still a mystery to me, and I keep hoping I'll come upon some gem-like insight that will explain it.

But not tonight.

WEDNESDAY, JANUARY 9

In the morning I decided to interview Dierdra Two Shoes's unpleasant mother and try to find out about the men her daughter had been running around with.

Mrs. Lagomarsino lived in a rented trailer in a small park on the western end of town. She was short and weighed two hundred pounds or more; in spite of the cold day, she'd covered her bulk with a flimsy pink-and-orange-and-green Hawaiian muumuu. When I stepped into her trailer, I understood the reason for the skimpy clothing: she had the heat in there cranked up to at least ninety degrees.

The room looked like a cyclone had hit a thrift shop: empty Southern Comfort bottles, cheap ceramic knickknacks, throw pillows, and full ashtrays were everywhere, many on the industrial-carpeted floor. Three cats peeked out at me from an adjoining door, then melted away, but their presence was still made known by the smell of an unclean litter box. Dorothy

Lagomarsino heaved herself into a dilapidated re-
cliner that wheezed when she put up the footrest. She
left it to me to remove a jumbled stack of blankets
from the love seat so I could sit down.

She lit a cigarette and said, "So you want to talk
about my whore of a daughter."

"I'm curious about her murder. I'm a Native
woman myself—"

"Why bother? Was no more than she deserved."

I studied her, trying to determine if she was actually that cold and uncaring or if her attitude was a
defensive pose to cover her loss.

Mrs. Lagomarsino added, "That girl should've
married Bart Upstream. But no, she didn't want to
be tied down to one man. She started going with
anybody in pants."

"The men she went with—who were they?"

"Uh-uh." She waggled a thick finger at me. "That
information is my insurance policy. What I know
keeps me alive and well fed."

"Keeps you alive? Aren't you afraid the same man
who killed your daughter might kill you?"

She didn't answer, just gave me a tight-lipped stare.

"You called Dierdra a whore," I said. "Why?"

"Because she was." The woman's voice dripped
bitterness. "My first husband, her father Two Shoes,
he left me when Dierdra was twelve. I caught my
second, Len Riskin, in bed with her three years later.
I threw both of them out, but the next year I took
her back. What's a mother to do when her only child
is homeless and starving? But while she was living
with me and Benny Lagomarsino, I found out she
was screwing around with him, the son of a bitch.

That was the last straw. They both went, and good riddance!"

"Was Dierdra involved with him when she was killed?"

"No. He got shot during a liquor store robbery not long after I threw his ass out. I didn't hear nothing about her until the cops came to the door and told me she was dead."

A depressing family saga, but no more so than most that clutter the pages of many a daily newspaper: "Father Kills Estranged Wife and Son, Then Self"; "Mom Drowns Children in Bathtub"; "Sister of mass murderer: 'He was the sweetest baby.'"

Sometimes I grow weary of the gloom and doom in the news and avoid the TV and Internet for days and let the newspapers pile up. Most of what I do read are the features and feel-good stories. I'll learn about the grim stuff soon enough, thank you.

There didn't seem to be anything more I could learn from Mrs. Lagomarsino, so I thanked Dierdra's mother for her time. She shrugged it off, but as I left I thought I saw a sheen of tears in her eyes; maybe Dorothy wasn't as callous as she wanted people to think.

12:18 p.m.

Back in the village, I had a not-very-good lunch at the Owl Cafe, then put in another call to the agency and asked for Mick. The line was even more staticky today. It made me glad I lived where cell-phone service was not only easily accessible but of a reliable quality.

Mick came on the line. "The vial got here safely and is at the lab," he said. "As far as the other stuff, this is only a partial list of the names you gave me, but here goes. Jake Blue: He studied biochemistry at Cal Poly at San Luis Obispo a few semesters, but didn't graduate. Has never married. Moved back to Meruk County after his sister was killed, been employed at the lumberyard there ever since. No criminal record, average credit rating. Kind of a nothing man."

That description didn't match the man who had spoken with such passion about his sister's murder, but the bare facts of a person's life often don't match what they're like inside.

"You said you had everything on Josie Blue," Mick went on, "but I found something that wasn't in the sheriff's file: She came back home because she had an unhappy love affair with a married man in Berkeley. A history professor named Max Kennedy. There aren't many details on him, but I'll keep checking."

Mick went on, ignoring my silence, as many years of working together had taught him to do. "Now the Harcourts. Ben Harcourt, the Old Man, is well connected. Folks in Sacramento and D.C. I'm having a hard time getting more on that, but Derek's working on it. He inherited the ranch from his father. Married late in life, to Victoria Spenser, whom he met while traveling in Australia. She gave him the two sons, died of pneumonia ten years ago.

"The sons: Kurt, the younger, has a master's in economics from Michigan, taught for a while at USC, but a few years ago he had a nervous breakdown and went home to help his father run the ranch."

"Can you get specifics on the breakdown?"

"Just that he spent time in a Napa sanatorium. Medically privileged information is difficult to access."

"What about Paul?"

"A successful businessman with a reputation as a playboy, a run-around stud."

"The reputation's justified—I've seen him in action. Any trouble with women? Particularly Native women?"

"Nope. He seems too smart for that. He's made a hell of a lot of money with his company, called Firestarter, and has been around, all over the world, and usually in the wrong places."

"Such as?"

"Vegas, Hong Kong—before the recent crises—Macao, South America. Places where gambling is a big business and, as well you know, things are not always what they seem."

"I think I'd better get some input from Hy on this. What about this company—Firestarter?"

"Its website claims it's an investment broker for—get this—'Those who wish to enjoy exceptional lives.' I'm checking with Luke at Merrill Lynch about its authenticity."

"Great. Keep on it. Did you get anything on Gene Byram and Vic Long?"

"Not much. They've worked as ranch hands for the Harcourts for about four years. Drifters with no fixed addresses before that. Neither of them has a record in Meruk County or anywhere else in California, but

Byram was arrested in Reno six years ago for attempted rape; charges were dropped when the woman left town."

"How about Sheriff Noah Arneson?"

"He's a homegrown boy—born and raised in Buford. He attended school there, went into the navy at eighteen, saw duty in San Antonio, Texas, and then in San Diego. Down there he was attached to the shore patrol, but was reassigned because of complaints of brutality."

"Who made the complaints?"

"Victims and witnesses both."

"Military witnesses?"

"Yes. Generally, naval witnesses of brutality don't protect their own."

I should've known that: my father had been a noncom in the navy much of his life. He would've reported Arneson too.

"Any more on him?" I asked Mick.

"He ended his naval career in purchasing—making deals for cheap soap and toothpaste for the post exchanges. That must've bored him, because when his tour of duty was up, he went back to Meruk County."

"How'd he get to be sheriff?"

"By being there at the right time. Nobody else wanted the job. And I guess they still don't, because he's been hanging on for eleven years now."

"Any indications of brutality?"

"Nothing more than what's typical in small-town jurisdictions. He beat up a high school kid, but the kid was supposedly attacking him with a lead pipe. Drew his gun on a bunch of men who were fighting in a bar, but they backed down and left. Shot the mayor's dog—claimed it was attacking him. Roughed up juveniles before returning them to their parents."

"But the potential for more violence is there. What about his personal life?"

"Married three times, divorced twice. Current wife's name is Abby."

"Grounds for the divorces?"

"Both no-fault. Although he did settle twenty thousand on the second wife."

"Meaning she had something on him."

"Probably. You need anything else—about the victims or their families?"

"Anything you can get."

"I'll see what I can find. Oh, I've got a message for you from Hank Zahn. He wants you to do him a favor. I told him you were out of town, but he asked me to give you the message when you checked in."

"What's the favor?"

"He wants you to talk with Habiba."

Hank Zahn was my best male friend since college days, my former boss from All Souls Legal Cooperative, and my lawyer. Habiba Hamid was Hank and his ex-wife's adopted twelve-year-old daughter. Hank had hinted that she wasn't dealing too well with the divorce, but things must have gotten worse since we'd last spoken.

I asked, "Why? Is something wrong?"

"Evidently. He said she'll tell you."

"When does he want me to call her?"

"ASAP. You have her cell number?"

"Yes."

12:50 p.m.

Habiba didn't recognize the number I was calling from, of course, but still she picked up immediately. "Shar," she said when she heard my voice, "oh my God, everything's going to hell."

We'd been in touch infrequently since her parents divorced, but when we did talk, she was usually upset. As seemed to be the case now.

"What's wrong?"

"They're driving me crazy!"

"Hank and Anne-Marie? What have they done now?"

"Anne-Marie's been offered a great job in Dallas. She wants to take me with her. Hank wants me to stay with him. They're talking custody suits."

I repressed a sigh. "What do *you* want?"

"Nobody's asked me."

"I am."

Pause. "Well, I'd rather things go on like they are now, but that's not possible. Dallas is . . . well, *icky*."

"Not really. It's a very cosmopolitan city."

"Don't give me that. It's in Texas."

"Texas has a fascinating history, and some of our best writers live there. McMurtry—"

"Who?"

"Larry McMurtry. He's a world-famous novelist and screenwriter. He won the Pulitzer Prize for *Lonesome Dove*, an epic about a cattle drive."

"Well, good for him, but cows are gross."

I gave up on that tack. "So you want to stay here?"

"There's a problem with that too—Hank's talking

about moving to Santa Barbara—some new woman he's got there. I love Anne-Marie, and I love Hank too. All my friends are here. My school is here. And if I tried to switch off between them, I'd spend all my time on airplanes. And I fuckin' hate to fly."

"You want me to talk to them?"

"Would you?"

McCone, the go-to girl for people with problems.

"Yes, but I can't right away. I'm in the middle of an investigation." And in no frame of mind to mediate a family dispute. "Are you staying with either of them?"

"No, with a friend from school. But I don't think her parents want me here."

"You've got a key to my house, right?"

"Yes."

"Take a cab there and move into the guest room. I don't know when I'll be back, but stay until we get things settled. Okay?"

"Okay. Thanks, Shar."

Shar—the go-to girl.

1:11 p.m.

Jake Blue was still nowhere to be found in Aspendale. There was nothing else for me to do in the village, and I wasn't ready to return to the shack, so I called Allie Foxx. Would it be possible to take her up on her previous offer of a tour of the rez? I asked. She responded in the affirmative: "I've gotta get out of this office!"

She picked me up in her Land Rover an hour later. On the way out of town I filled her in on what I'd learned so far.

She asked, "Do you think Jake Blue may be involved with these murders?"

"No, not directly. Unless his sister's murder four years ago is somehow connected. He thinks one of the Harcourt brothers may be involved."

"Wouldn't surprise me. The Harcourts are elitists—they do pretty much whatever they want to."

"But killing?"

"Who knows? Those people will do anything to preserve their status and power."

We sped across barren land dotted with boulders, shadowed patches of snow, and winter-dead vegetation. In the distance, jagged peaks thrust upward into banks of low-hanging clouds. The afternoon felt heavy, oppressive. I opened my window slightly to let in the cold air.

Allie said, "This land was gifted to us by the 'generosity' of the US government—never mind that they stole it from us in the first place. First I'm going to take you on a short tour, then we'll go see Mamie Louise. She's an auntie of mine."

Nothing marked the entrance to the reservation. A dirt road veered off the highway through scrub cacti and more dead vegetation. After about half a mile it ended at some weathered wooden barriers where a number of beater cars and trucks were parked.

Allie said, "From here on, we travel by foot."

"Nobody drives in?"

"Very few, except for delivery trucks. There's a history of flash floods here."

Great. Acres of barren land, few services, and the possibility of drowning. This is what they gave the Natives.

We skirted the other vehicles and moved along a narrow track that looked beaten down by generations of feet. The sky was a mottled gray, clouds rolling in, but when I asked Allie about the prospect of rain or snow, she shook her head. "The storm clouds'll drift southeast, end up in Nevada."

Buildings began to appear: a few plywood shacks, a scattering of prefabs of different ages and states of repair, a pair of old log cabins. Directly ahead of us was a low cinder-block structure flying a flag I didn't recognize.

Allie said, "That's the Meruk Nation Hall and convenience store. We've got no medical services on the rez, but a doctor and a couple of nurses volunteer to come in every two weeks or so and hold a clinic there."

"What if somebody has a serious health problem or needs emergency assistance?"

"Serious problems have to be treated in Alturas or Crescent City, even as far away as Santa Rosa. It means a helicopter ride. As for other emergencies"—she shrugged—"you hope for a response."

I looked up at the flag on the Meruk Nation Hall. It depicted thin, black, dancing figures against a wavy background of fiery orange, bright blue, and magenta.

When I asked her about the flag, Allie replied, "It depicts the Three Warriors—an important part of Meruk legend."

"The warriors look to be women."

"They very well could be. We're a matriarchal

tribe. Most are. Stems from the days when the males went out hunting and were never home. Women had to control the home and the land. They were the decision-makers. Some even fought in wars."

I was about to ask her more when I saw a woman approaching us—short, nearly bald, with nut-brown skin and a big smile. She walked with an intricately carved cane, and her clothing was brilliant—not in the hues of the Meruk flag, but in the shiny turquoise and pink polyester offerings of Walmart.

"Auntie," Allie called.

The woman's smile grew wider, revealing gapped teeth. "'Bout time you came to see me, you rascal," she said. "Who's this with you?"

"A friend from San Francisco, Sharon McCone. She's come to see the rez."

Mamie Louise stared at me, eyes narrowed. "She looks like the city, but part of her belongs here. What's your tribe, girl?"

"Shoshone." The clan was what Elwood had told me; I suspected he'd made it up. My birth father had spent many years in New York, only returning when his wife, a member of the Blackfeet Nation, wanted to get back to her roots. Elwood in many ways was as citified as any of Manhattan's residents.

Mamie Louise considered. "Good people, them Shoshones. Too proud of their horses, but otherwise good." She turned her gaze to Allie. "You just lookin' around, huh?"

"That's right."

"Hmmm. Well, look all you like, and then you come back to my house for tea."

As we walked away, Allie whispered to me, "Be

prepared. She makes the most horrible tea in the West—bark, roots, wild berries, strange plants. It's a wonder she hasn't killed anybody yet."

"She seems somewhat formidable."

"She is. On this rez there are three Warrior Women, a title that's passed down from generation to generation. They're tough as nails, and they rule. Absolutely nothing happens here without their official okay. She may seem like a dotty old lady, but Mamie Louise is the strongest of all."

3:38 p.m.

Mamie Louise's tea *was* horrible—but the rez was worse. Children played in the hardscrabble soil, as children the world over do, blissfully ignorant of the difficult lives they faced in the future. A few women gathered around a metal drum, washing clothes; their movements were slow and heavy, and they regarded Allie and me listlessly as we passed.

Mamie Louise had prepared a tea tray on her rickety kitchen table: three kinds of brew and a plate of oatmeal cookies that her next-door neighbor had baked. The cookies helped tame the taste of the tea. And Mamie's joy at having visitors turned the gathering into a special occasion.

She chattered about the rez. "Once this was beautiful country. I came here as a bride with my first husband, who I met over in Idaho, where I was born. Our girls, they both died as babies. Measles, nobody ever vaccinated here. For a while we talked about going someplace else, where they treated you like human beings, but the time just passed...My husband, he died in a tractor accident on a ranch where he was working. My next man, he went off, looking for lively times in the big city. There were others, but nobody that really counted."

"Are you glad you stayed here?" I asked.

"Yeah, sure. It's home. I got my government allotment. I got my say in local matters. Besides, where would I go? No family, no friends except who's here. Although I sometimes get visitors. More of them than ever lately."

That caught my attention. "Oh, who?"

She sat up straighter, looking proud. "Some of the finest white folk around here. Mr. Paul Harcourt—you know those people?"

I nodded.

"He brought me two bags of fertilizer for my vegetable garden and promised to come back and dig it into the soil. And that man who owns the lumberyard—what's his name? Well, no matter. He stopped by and helped me make plans for a chicken coop. I haven't had chickens for years, and I do like fresh eggs. He said he'd bring me the materials at no cost." She turned shining eyes to me. "Ain't it wonderful, what the good people in the world will do?"

5:10 p.m.

"'Ain't it wonderful?'" I said to Allie as we sped back toward Aspendale.

"It ain't. Something bad is going on around here."

"You mean you don't believe millionaires are eager to build chicken coops for indigent old lady Natives?"

She snorted. "No. And I don't just mean the murders."

We rode in silence for a time. Then the cell in my pocket buzzed, something of a surprise because the only people who had the number were the Sisters and Mick.

It was Mick, sounding distressed. The line was fairly clear this time, clear enough for me to hear chaotic noise in the background—raised voices, furniture scraping. "Shar, I've got some bad news. There's been a shooting here—"

"What?"

"Some nut with a semiautomatic pistol busted in— I don't know how he got past all our security—and started firing. Ted was the only one who got hit."

Oh my God.

"Ted...He's not..."

"No, he's all right. Just a flesh wound in his shoulder. Pure luck that nobody else was hurt, but everybody's pretty badly shaken up."

"What about the shooter?"

"One of the security guards heard the shots, rushed in, and blew him away. No ID on him yet. You're going to need to come down, deal with the cops and insurance people."

"I'll be there as soon as I can."

When I blurted out the news to Allie Foxx, she drove me straight to the airstrip. Hal Bascomb, whom I called as we drove, had my plane fueled and ready to go.

The flight seemed to take forever. I was badly upset by the news; I couldn't imagine what had triggered the attack. And I feared for Ted, my forever friend...

My landing at North Field was less than stellar, but I didn't think I'd record it as such in my logbook.

I reclaimed my car from where I'd parked it near the tie-downs and headed for the Bay Bridge. Traffic was snarled in spite of its being past the rush hour, and I cursed all the way into the city.

7:01 p.m.

By the time I arrived at our building, only one police car was still on the street, and any onlookers had long since been dispersed. Shards of broken glass from our triple-paned windows glittered on the sidewalk. A uniformed cop stood guard at the entrance, and when I showed him my ID, he allowed me into the underground parking garage. The one elevator that was working took a long time to get to our floor.

There were armed security guards by the elevator; they knew me and waved me inside. Furniture had been tipped over, items on the desks knocked askew. My eyes were drawn to a huge blood spatter on the carpet—the shooter's, evidently, where the guard had shot him. Two bullet holes marred the wall behind the reception desk; more slugs had ripped down the hallway, past other cubicles, and taken out a Plexiglas partition around Ted's domain.

A heavy silence filled the suite. Mick appeared when I called out, put his arms around me, and held me close.

I asked, "Ted?"

"Being treated at SF General."

"Everybody else?"

"They're shaken but okay. I sent them home."

"Has the shooter been ID'd yet?"

"Not yet. The detectives seem to think he might be connected with Hy's work in Mexico."

"Hy—does he know what happened?"

"He knows. I got hold of him right after I talked to you."

"Is he coming back?"

"As soon as he can."

I let go of Mick, straightened. "Where was Ted when the shooter broke in?" I asked.

"Just coming down the hallway. The first shot got him in the shoulder, the second missed entirely."

"Thank God for that."

"There's an SFPD cop who wants to talk with you. I put his number on your desk."

"Okay, I'll deal with it."

I went into my office, dumped my bags on my desk, and sat down on one of the chairs in the seating area that overlooked the Bay. Fog had been streaming in as I'd landed at Oakland, and now all I could see was a blank gray wall.

9:15 p.m.

I made short work of the phone interview with the homicide cop, an inspector named Frank Baker. No, I had no enemies who would have retaliated in such a blatant way. Did my husband? I didn't know; we kept our investigations separate. Where was he? On his way from Mexico. Where had I been at the time of the attack? In Meruk County, working a case. What case? That's confidential. We need to know, Ms. McCone. I need to talk with my attorney, Inspector Baker.

9:30 p.m.

I tried to call Hy but got no answer on his cell. I left a voice mail message. Next I called the hospital to check on Ted. Good news: he'd been released an hour before in the care of his husband, Neal Osborn.

Hank, my attorney and close friend, was third on my list. He'd already heard what had happened and sounded shaken. I told him about my conversation with Inspector Baker, and he said he'd talk to Baker and negotiate a convenient time for a phone interview with me.

Then he asked, "Have you talked with Habiba?"

"Yes. Don't you think you've treated her shabbily? You don't take a child into your life and just toss her aside when it's inconvenient."

"I know that, but—"

"I've said my piece. Do what your conscience dictates. And now I've got to go."

When I called Ted's home, Neal answered and said he was resting comfortably.

"Is he in pain?" I asked. "Badly upset?"

"He's still flying high on a shot they gave him at the hospital. So no pain. No upset either—he thinks of himself as a hero."

"Well, give the hero my love, and tell him I'll come see him tomorrow."

10:05 p.m.

Exhausted, I went home to my house on Avila Street in the Marina district.

The house is on a corner lot, Spanish Revival style, and Hy and I had been lucky to buy it just before the real estate prices in San Francisco went berserk. The tech boom in Silicon Valley had lured many young instant multimillionaires into the city, and they bought and bought and bought without any understanding of what property was actually worth. As a result we have a ton of overvalued homes that will go for pennies on the dollar if and when the tech bubble bursts.

I left my car in the driveway and let myself in by the front door. The house was still warm from the afternoon sun, and totally silent. Then I heard the sound that Hy and I call "thundering cat hooves," and two black furballs tumbled down the stairway. Alex and Jessie launched themselves at me, purring and mowling and rubbing against my legs. Jessie gave me love bites through my jeans.

"Okay, take it easy, you guys." I followed them into the kitchen and refilled their bowls with kibble and water, poured myself a glass of Deer Hill Chardonnay, sat at the table, and watched as they scarfed up their meal.

There was no evidence that Habiba had been here. Maybe she'd changed her mind about accepting my invitation. If she did move in, I hoped she wouldn't be planning on a long stay. For a while we'd had a young friend, Chelle Curley, and her cat living with us. But Chelle, a rehabber of old houses, had found one that she wanted for her own and was now living across town in Ashbury Heights. Chelle hadn't been with us long, but even so the house had seemed crowded.

After a while I relaxed enough to check my personal voice mail messages, all of which had been left before the shooting at M&R.

My birth father, Elwood, calling from the Flathead Reservation in Montana. "Daughter, I am doing as you advised me—calling more often. When you assemble your thoughts, please call back."

My birth mother, Saskia Blackhawk, an attorney in Boise. "Sharon, Elwood's worried about you, and he's driving me crazy. Do something about him!"

I smiled, glad they were close enough that he could pester her with his worries. Elwood and Saskia had a one-night stand during a visit she made to the rez that resulted in my conception, but she—a student with very little money—decided to put me up for adoption. My adoptive parents, distant relatives of hers, raised me as one of theirs—in hindsight a bad decision because I was a dark-skinned and -haired child amid four blond Scotch-Irish siblings. As proof of my superior detecting abilities, I fell for their story that I was a genetic throwback until my thirties, when the truth finally came out.

Now we were all family. I'd learned that I had a half sister, Robin Blackhawk, an attorney here in the city, and a half brother, Darcy. Robin had become a good friend, but Darcy was the problem child, having worn out his welcome at most of the facilities for schizophrenics west of the Mississippi. Saskia, Robin, and I periodically obsessed about what we'd do with him next, then decided that we'd march on east.

There were also messages from my sister Patsy, who was about to open her third restaurant—in Sonoma County, which meant she was getting closer to me year by year. My friend Carolina Owens, just to chat. My niece Jamie, a performer like her father, Ricky Savage, asking me to attend a concert she'd been part of in San Jose last night. Another friend, Linnea Carraway, a TV newscaster in Seattle, excited about a promotion.

I considered keeping the recording to replay when I was feeling alone and unloved.

Mick called several minutes later. "About that sample your pilot friend brought me. I just heard from the guy who works nights at a lab I took it to. The stuff is called Arbritazone, a rare earth element—a powerful antipsychotic drug and sedative, administered in only the most extreme cases. Doctors who prescribe it are mainly psychiatrists, but there's also a large black market for it, as there is for most psychoactive drugs."

Why would Jake have had such a drug? I'd seen

nothing in his background that would indicate he was consulting a psychiatrist. Had he gotten it on the black market? Why?

"Can you track down the sample's source?"

"I'll try. But I bet nobody is going to own up to it. Not putting the patient's or doctor's name on a prescription is a no-no in this state."

10:25 p.m.

The doorbell rang. Now who could that be at this hour? My address is not publicly available, but in this technological age there's no such thing as privacy. Anybody can find out pretty much anything about anybody on the Internet.

The ringing continued. I went to the door, thinking it might be Habiba, but then a familiar male voice called out to me: my symbolic cousin, Will Camphouse. He held a miniature white rose plant in one hand, a bottle of wine in the other.

"I heard what went on at the agency," he said, "and thought you might be in need of some cheer."

"Thank you." I hugged him, ushered him in. "It's all over the news, right?"

"Yeah. You have any idea what that bastard's motive was?"

"No, I can't figure it. The cops assume it was linked to one of Hy's cases. He may know when he gets back from Mexico."

"Crazy business. Where were you when it happened?"

"Meruk County. I came back because of the attack. And I'm not getting anywhere on the case I'm working up there."

"So you're staying down here permanently?"

"No. I'll be going back up there pretty soon."

"Well, you look like you could use a snort right now." He brandished the wine bottle.

"You've always been so elegant with words. And thank you for the roses."

"I know yellow roses are Hy's purview," he said, "so I thought white might be better." He was referring to my husband's longtime practice of sending me a single yellow rose—my favorite—every Tuesday morning, a Tuesday being the day we'd met.

"They're perfect. I have an empty space in the garden just waiting for them."

Will and I had encountered one another on the Flathead Reservation in Montana when I'd first gone there to meet Elwood. We struck up a friendship and tried to figure out if we were related. Native bloodlines being as tangled as they are, we finally gave up and decided we were cousins, if only symbolically. At the time Will had been visiting the rez and working at an ad agency in Tucson; later he'd moved to San Francisco and opened his own firm. What with my brother John and former brother-in-law, Ricky, having moved here, and Patsy getting closer every year, I felt as if I'd become a pivotal point for the entire family. Which can be…well, good or bad, depending on who's on good terms and who's feuding with whom.

I went to the kitchen, opened his wine, fetched glasses. Will settled onto the sofa in front of the fireplace, and I knelt and stirred the wood until the flames flared.

He said, "The case you're working on concerns the murder of those two Native women?"

"Yes. The reason I'm not getting anywhere is the atmosphere up there—it's toxic."

"In what way?"

"Hard to put into words. All these rumors float-ing around about the murders, but few people are willing to talk about them. Law enforcement that's antagonistic to Natives. Rich ranchers who are after something, but I can't figure what."

Will took a swallow of wine. "Killings of Native women aren't confined to Meruk County—they've been going on for twenty years or more and extend north into Canada. There was a recent statement from Prime Minister Trudeau that the Canadian gov-ernment is beginning a stepped-up investigation of them. Also, the US attorney general has announced a nationwide plan—the Missing and Murdered Indige-nous Persons Initiative—that would involve the FBI in investigating the cases."

"Wish somebody would step it up in California." I set the poker down and leaned against the over-stuffed chair next to the fireplace. "In Meruk County there seems to be a prevailing attitude among law en-forcement officials that crimes involving Natives don't matter. Every time I come up against a mind-set like that, I realize we're not the humanitarians we pride ourselves on being."

"Well, since the murders and disappearances have been going on for twenty or more years, they can't be linked to the same perp or perps. The Canadian crimes were the first—who knows how many. Next, two murders and an indeterminate number of disappearances in Washington state, a murder in Oregon, and ten reported disappearances. The two in Meruk are only the most recent. Any more disappearances up there recently?"

"One that I know of, five days ago. She could be victim number three."

"So if you confine these crimes to the United States, you have an indefinite number of Native women disappearing over, say, a twenty-year period. I wonder if there are any international statistics." Will drank again, looking grimly thoughtful. Then he took out his phone.

"Who are you calling?"

"Friend of mine back east."

"It's way past midnight there—"

He waved for me to be silent. "Hey, Lily," he said into the phone. "I know it's late, but... Well, right, you old night owl."

I listened as Will explained the situation.

"If you can run those figures, I'd appreciate it," he said. "There's a case of that wine you like from St. Francis in it for you... Yeah, love you too. I'll wait to hear."

"*Love* you?" I asked when he disconnected, raising my eyebrows.

"An old friend with benefits. Lily's an analyst at Quantico; she doesn't pass on sensitive information, but I doubt what I'm asking her is anything the papers wouldn't be able to find out and print if they found it newsworthy."

"But they don't bother to print it. Natives, you know."

"Yeah."

We sat mostly silent for a while, listening to the crackle and pop of the fire.

Half an hour later his phone rang. He listened, then said, "That's too bad. Can you access any more on the individual cases? Anything about the legislative crap? ... Yeah, I can wait awhile; this stuff's been going on for generations, but McCone and I would sure like to shine some light on it soon. Also, there's this Indian Restitution Organization...They aren't? Well, that's good. Thanks, love. Talk soon."

He closed the phone. "The Restitution Organization's defunct. Lily feels there's been a lock put on the information about these cases, but she'll keep trying and e-mail me what she already knows. You hungry?"

"I don't remember when I last ate."

"Cheeseburgers? Greasy old curly fries? Other stuff that the health police would arrest us for?"

I nodded.

He opened his phone again. "I happen to have an app for twenty-four-hour home delivery of just those things."

11:52 p.m.

"So," Will said, munching on a cheeseburger, "Native women in all types of communities—cities, suburbia, country, and reservations—are murdered at ten times the national average. As for disappearances, there aren't any accurate records, but it's thought to number in the thousands over the past fifty years." Lily had just e-mailed him the promised reports.

"Do they say what that's attributable to?" As if I didn't know.

"Poor response from law enforcement agencies, as you've seen up in Meruk. Prosecutors have declined to pursue around fifty-two percent of crimes against Natives. Then there're the legal loopholes, such as the one that allows non-Native offenders immunity from crimes they commit on Indigenous lands."

"How can they do that?"

"Once the perps are off the rez, they aren't culpable. It's the law—made by whites."

"That sucks." I dipped a fry in ketchup, looked at it, and put it back on my plate.

"Yeah, it does. There's a nationally based organization similar to your Sisters—the Missing and Murdered Indigenous Women. You know about them?"

"Yes. The Sisters told me and I checked their website." I yawned. "I'm running out of steam, Will. Let's call it a night."

"Sure. You go upstairs, get some sleep. I'll clean up and let myself out."

I went up and checked the guest room to see if Habiba was there.

She wasn't, but her stuff was piled around. So at least for a while, we had a boarder. Then I took Will's advice and went to bed.

THURSDAY, JANUARY 10

8:40 a.m.

Another call from Mick, this one dragging me out of sleep. The first thing he said was, "You going back to that godforsaken county today?"

Half-awake, I could only grunt at him.

"I mean, I've arranged an appointment for you in Berkeley if you can haul your ass out of bed."

"Where in Berkeley?"

"Telegraph Avenue and Bancroft Way. Subject's meeting you on the northwest corner."

"What subject? Who?"

"Guy called Max Kennedy, Josie Blue's former boyfriend. I located him as you asked, and he's willing to talk to you."

"Kind of tight for parking around there."

"If you pick me up, I can just go around the block a couple of times; it shouldn't take you more than fifteen minutes."

"All right. What time?"

"The meeting's at ten o'clock. Better hurry."

10:02 a.m.

Mick drove my car to Berkeley after I picked him up. My nephew is over six feet and handsome like his father, blond like his mother, and we both harbor some amusing memories of our times together. Two of them he claims have emotionally scarred him for all eternity. The first is when I dropped him on his head while babysitting. (He was okay, just screamed for a while.) And the second is when I threatened to kill him if he didn't pick up his toys. (He picked them up, then threw them out an upstairs window when my back was turned. Since he didn't believe my threats when he was four, I've never used that ploy again.)

Today he seemed in an unusually bad mood. "Look at this weather," he grumbled. "January—the hell with it. I wish we could skip the whole month."

"But then there's February."

"Yeah. And March."

"Well, February at least has Valentine's Day."

"For you it does."

I smiled; I'd been waiting for an opportunity to find out how his love life was going.

"Shar, why are you doing that?"

"Doing what?"

"That thing that you do with your face when you're trying to drag information out of me. Sometimes I feel like a suspect in a police interrogation."

"Have you done anything that would make you a suspect?"

"Dammit, stop it! You're so nosy...Okay, Naomi

and I broke up. Two weeks ago. So I don't have any-body to celebrate Valentine's Day with."

"What happened?" I liked Naomi, a teacher who worked with disabled kids in the local school district.

"The usual—she found somebody else."

Over the years Mick has had a string of women friends, including a couple that I'd thought might be long term, but none lasted. His irregular hours, lack of elementary skills such as cooking and clean-ing, and excessive devotion to televised sports had all been cited as reasons for the breakups. But I suspected it was something else: Mick didn't relate on an emotional level.

He'd been deeply scarred by the overly publicized end of his parents' marriage as well as his father's union with Rae, whom he'd previously thought of as his friend and colleague. He'd felt a responsibility for his five siblings, but they'd proved resilient to the turmoil in their young lives. The home he'd bought on Potrero Hill had been vandalized by a criminal who had taken it to be mine.

Now he owned a condo in one of the new South Beach high-rises, a few floors above his uncle, my older brother, John. But John said he seldom saw him, unless he sought him out. His mother and her new husband were currently living in London and had re-peatedly asked him to visit, but he'd put them off.

Mick had built himself an impenetrable cocoon. I wondered what it would take to lure him out of it.

"I'm sorry about the breakup," I said.

"When it's over, it's over."

When we reached the appointed corner in Berkeley, I hopped out and was met by a red-haired man in a blue scarf and brown overcoat. Max Kennedy, the history professor who had been Josie Blue's lover.

"Ms. McCone." He clasped my hand with strong fingers.

"Is there someplace we can talk privately?"

He motioned to a coffee shop halfway down the block on Telegraph. Beanz & Greenz. We went inside and claimed a small table by a front window. While Max Kennedy went up to the counter to fetch coffees, I stared out at the ebb and flow of people on the avenue. This was once my territory, where I'd walked to and from classes with my friends. It hadn't changed much, just the names on the businesses and the students, who looked far too young to be in college. But then I supposed I'd looked that young once.

I'd loved the campus the first time I'd set eyes on it: the Campanile, Memorial Glade, Sather Gate, Memorial Stadium. To me it was the fulfillment of a dream, a place where I could learn and be free of a confining and mostly chaotic home life.

College hadn't been a carefree romp, however. True, I'd lived with an ever-changing cast of roommates in a large, brown-shingled house on Durant Avenue, where we'd indulged in the usual parties and illegal substances and romantic entanglements. But I'd had to struggle financially, even with my scholarship— my family couldn't afford to help with expenses—and had ended up working many evenings as a security guard in various office buildings in San Francisco. Of course, the buildings were all wired with the most sophisticated systems then available, and the guard in the lobby was just window dressing; I'd never been threatened, and in the quiet nights, I got a hell of a lot of studying done. Enough that I'd graduated with honors.

Max Kennedy came back with the coffee. "Sorry I took so long. It's a madhouse up by the counter."

"No problem. I was just sitting here watching ghosts of my college days wander by."

"Ah, you're an alumna." He looked at me with more respect.

Academics are odd that way: they think a degree confers special status upon a person. In my opinion it's the former students' abilities and how they use their learning that confer status. For years I'd considered my BA in sociology to be something they handed out as a reward for good test-taking abilities and being able to sit still even in the most boring lectures and seminars. But as time passed, I found that I'd developed an understanding of people, groups, and situations that I might not otherwise have had. And such an understanding is what an investigator thrives on.

When I didn't come forth with a ringing endorsement of my alma mater—which would have substantially lengthened our conversation—Professor Kennedy said, "I understand you want to talk to me about Josie Blue."

I shook my head to clear it of the memories. "Sorry. It's always a little disorienting to come back here. Josie was a student of yours?"

"Only for a history class that's required for teacher certification. I met her there and then ran into her at a party about six months later."

"Isn't there a prohibition against dating students?"

"Dating students in one's classes, yes. Otherwise..." He shrugged.

"So you dated for...?"

"The rest of that academic year. Then we moved in together. But late in her junior year she met up with some Native students and began talking about getting back to her roots. It started innocently enough: she studied up on crafts, organized a show of her beadwork, took some classes. But then she hooked up with this group that had a reputation for violent protests. She moved out on me, and from then on she was with them 24-7."

"Tell me about the group."

"The Indigenous Restitution Organization. They're no longer in existence. They joined another group in a protest somewhere, I think at UC Davis, and there was a shooting. The other group's leader was killed, and after that... Well, they may have gone underground, I don't know."

"And Josie?"

"She went home after graduation, and I never heard from her again, except for a text apologizing for our breakup and saying that she'd found her true love in Meruk County."

"She give any hint as to who that was?"

"No. I'm wondering if it was a who or a what. I mean, maybe she came to identify more with the county after being away so long."

"Was Josie the sort of woman who would feel that way?"

He hesitated, then shook his head. "You know, for all the time we spent together, I never really knew what went on in her head. She had a reserve that I couldn't get past. She was easy to talk with, but afterwards I couldn't quite grasp what we'd talked about. You know what I mean?"

In certain circumstances I'd employed such a reserve myself. "I do," I said, "I know exactly what you mean."

11:29 a.m.

Mick picked me up on the same corner and slid over to let me drive. "Anything?" he asked.

"Josie was in love with someone in Meruk—or maybe just the county itself." I explained about the text she'd sent to Max Kennedy.

"Cryptic," he said. "Anything else?"

"That's about it."

"Where to now?"

"I want to see Ted. Considering the mess at the agency, I assume you want to work from home?"

"Yeah. Drop me at my building."

12:20 p.m.

Ted and Neal lived on Plum Alley, high on the northeastern side of Telegraph Hill, in a classic art deco apartment building. There was a rounded glass-block elevator at one corner and a number of boldly colored art-glass windows staggered at intervals across the façade. As I walked past them on

the second-floor level, I thought of how the crea-
tures they depicted reminded me of fantastical sea
serpents.

Neal answered the door in a red terry bathrobe. I
didn't believe I'd ever seen him so casual.

"How's he doing?" I asked.

"Grumpy, is how he's doing. I think he'd rather be
back in the hospital being fawned over."

Neal looked tired. Difficult patients were outside
the realm of his expertise.

"Where is he?"

"Upstairs. He's all yours."

Like the building, the apartment was dramatic:
two levels, with expansive Bay views and a curving
staircase that rose to a chrome-railed catwalk that led
between the bedrooms. Neal and Ted had preserved
the building's past in their choice of furnishings:
thirties-style sofa and armchairs and ottomans in
subdued colors. It was like stepping back in time—
except for the sound of Bruce Springsteen's voice
coming from a speaker.

I went up the stairs, crossed the catwalk to the
rear bedroom. Ted lay on the king-size bed on top of
a blue comforter, his shoulder bandaged. He wore a
garish bright-yellow caftan.

"Nice duds," I said.

"I hate them. I look stupid."

He did, but I didn't confirm his judgment. Instead
I placed a box of the peanut brittle he likes on his
bedside table.

"Are you willing to talk about the shooting? I know
you've already gone over it with the police, but…"

"Wasn't much I could tell them. I was going over

some spreadsheets—tax time coming up soon—and I heard a strange sound down by the reception area, went to see what was going on, and then felt a sharp pain and passed out."

"Did you see the shooter?"

"Just a blur of black—his clothing, I guess."

"Anything else?"

He shook his head.

"Okay, to change the subject—why are you wearing that caftan if you hate it?"

He sighed. "It's the only fashion statement I can think of to make. Neal suggested it, but I can tell he doesn't like it on me. In fact, he hinted that he's beginning to find my changes of dress wearying."

"Sounds like you might be too."

"...Maybe. That Botany 500 stage went on way too long. After a while I started thinking like Mannix." The private detective character in the 1970s TV crime show who had always sported the then-popular menswear.

"Oh? In what way?"

"Suspicious and angry." Ted's lips twisted, and I waited.

"Maybe," he finally said, "I'm just afraid of growing up."

I considered that. Ted and I, like many of our friends, come from a generation of sometimes child-like eccentrics. It had taken me a long time to realize that a well-tailored business suit presents a better image to clients than faded jeans. I'd had difficulty imagining myself owning a home, getting married, or managing a business. But then I'd realized those were only superficial changes; I'd always be the same person I was inside—quirky behavior, weird sense of humor, occasional acts of lunacy.

I said, "Don't grow up, just fake it. Don't lose the caftans or the Botany stuff or your Hawaiian and Edwardian getups. That's what closets are for."

"Yeah, but then what do I wear?"

"Ask Neal. He likes to dress—and undress—you."

2:05 p.m.

The agency struck me as an eerie, alien place. Even with the furnace on, the suite felt cold, and I could hear the wind whistling around the plastic tarps that had been taped over the broken windows. The blood and shards of glass had been cleaned up, but the bullet holes were still stark reminders of the shooting.

I was on the way down the hallway to my office when Derek Frye came out of his office and told me the shooter had been identified. His name was Evan McCarthy, a drifter originally from Tennessee. His motive was not apparent, but he'd been carrying two thousand dollars in cash, an indication that he might have been paid for his rampage. SFPD was checking on his connections and recent whereabouts.

I googled McCarthy but found nothing but a list of similar names, none of them from Tennessee. A welcome call from Hy came just as I finished. Some sort of problem had held up his departure from Mexico, but his scheduled flight home would be leaving soon. It was the first I'd heard from him in quite a while, and I was relieved that he was all right. Given our often hazardous professions, our phone conversations were lifelines.

"They've identified the shooter," I told him, "a drifter named Evan McCarthy. Does the name ring any bells?"

"No. Never heard of him."

"He had two thousand dollars on him. Paid to go after somebody in the agency, maybe—you, or me."

"Better me than you. What do the police think?"

"Nothing definite, they're still investigating. Any idea who may have hired him?"

"None. If there's a connection here in Mexico, I can't imagine what it is. Could be something out of the past, if he was hired. Our firm has made a good many enemies over the years."

"We need to beef up security in this building."

"Yes, we do. How did McCarthy get in?"

"One of the guards must have been away from his post and isn't admitting it. The guard on our floor—Bendix—was the one who spotted and shot him."

"We'll talk about it when I get there."

"If I'm still here by then. I've got to fly back to Meruk County pretty soon."

"Making any headway up there?"

"Some. Not enough."

"Well, do what you have to do. I'll see you whenever."

After I finished talking to Hy, I decided I'd better return the calls I'd found on my home machine from Elwood and Saskia. They were bound to be worried if they didn't hear from me.

"Daughter," Elwood said, "I spoke with young Will earlier. He says there was a shooting by a crazed intruder in your offices and one of your employees was wounded."

I should have sworn Will to secrecy.

"Ted, my office manager. His wound isn't serious, fortunately. No one else was hurt."

"You must take steps to see that no such incident happens again."

"Don't worry, we intend to."

After a pause Elwood said, "Will also told me you are investigating some trouble on a reservation in a far northern county."

"It's just a bit of historical research."

"Do not lie to me. It concerns the death of thousands of Native women."

"No, only two."

"Do not make me say bullshit."

"You've already said it."

"So I have. But you must understand—this is not an isolated problem. We have had it here in Montana too. You may have seen that the attorney general has announced he is addressing the problem. It has been going on for many years—twenty or more. I have put out inquiries on the moccasin telegraph. You will be receiving their e-mail reports soon."

"The moccasin telegraph is *online*?"

"Perhaps because you were raised white, you think we are still sending smoke signals into the sky?"

"No, but are *you* online?"

"Elwoodtheartist@blackfoot.com."

I was stunned. Silent.

Elwood said, "We old farts get around too."

2:15 p.m.

Saskia's private line was busy for some time. When I finally reached her, I said, "Have you been talking to Elwood, by any chance?"

"Yes. He was quite concerned about your safety. I learned of the shooting on CNN and am concerned as well."

"You needn't be. I was out of the city when it happened."

"Yes, I know. Do the police have any leads on the perpetrator?"

I explained that the shooter had been identified and that the police were trying to establish a motive. I also said that I had spoken to Elwood and reassured him. "Does he really have an e-mail address?" I asked then.

"Yes."

"I didn't even know he had a computer."

"He took some classes at the junior college last fall, and then he went out and bought an Apple."

I tried to imagine a computer setup in my father's old cabin on the rez, then shrugged it off. Life is full of contrasts.

"The times are changing, Sharon," Saskia added.

"Funny, but I'm not adapting to the changes as well as most of you older people are."

"Well, I could say we adapt better because we've attained wisdom, but that's an old saw. Many people of my age are doddering around, repeating lifelong mistakes. The rest of us…well, we don't care to be that way. I think you've adapted to change very well, but haven't taken the time to slow down and appreciate it."

"You're probably right."

Saskia changed the subject by saying that Will had told her of my investigation in Meruk County. I gave her a brief account of the case to date, then said, "I need to ask you some questions about Native allotments."

"What has that to do with your investigation?"

"I'm not sure, but I sense it does."

"Then trust your intuition. Shall I give you a brief rundown?"

"Please."

"The allotments began in 1887 with the Dawes Act, otherwise known as the General Allotment Act, which made the Bureau of Indian Affairs responsible for Natives' financial welfare. Ostensibly the thrust of the legislation was to bring the tribes into the country's system of land ownership, but the desired result was the usurping of nearly one hundred million acres of tribal land by whites."

"My God! Which tribes were most affected?"

"The Curtis Act of 1898 names what were then called the Five Civilized Tribes: Cherokee, Chickasaw, Choctaw, Creek, and Seminole. Through the years, the list was expanded."

"But the land ended up belonging to whites."

"Much of it. The Natives didn't want to abandon their way of living, and they resisted, but eventually the government forced them to sell out. There are still some allotments within various reservations held in trust by the government, although the laws were abolished in 1934."

"But either way, the Natives got screwed again."

She sighed. "Old story. Is there anything else you need to know?"

"Not at the moment. I've been in touch with Robin, but how's Darcy?"

"Another old story. He's not doing well in his new group home. Robin and I are already looking for another place to move him when he commits some atrocity to make the new place reject him. We've decided perhaps somewhere in the Midwest—where his reputation hasn't preceded him."

"What about when you run out of the Midwest?"

"Then we start on the East Coast. Maybe Europe. Who knows?"

We talked of less consequential things, and after we finished our conversation, I thought about the fortunate people: people who were accomplished, educated, had their lives together. Many outsiders would suppose Saskia, a high-powered attorney who had successfully argued for Indigenous rights before the Supreme Court, led a charmed life. But then, outsiders didn't know Darcy.

2:40 p.m.

My head ached, possibly due to the switch between the pure air of Meruk County and the smog that hovered over the Bay today. I had just finished taking two aspirin when Derek appeared, signaling from the doorway that I should pick up on line two.

A woman's voice said, "My name is Alicia Jordan.

I'm a doctor in the emergency room at Santa Rosa Memorial."

"What can I do for you, Dr. Jordan?"

"A young female was airlifted in yesterday afternoon, badly traumatized. I'm Meruk, and the patient appears to be too, so I contacted the Sisters, thinking it might be something they should look into. Allie Foxx referred me to you."

"What happened to your patient?"

"Multiple injuries. She'd been sexually assaulted, beaten, and she may lose the sight in her right eye."

The words made me grimace with anger. "Who did this to her?"

"We don't know."

"Where was she found?"

"The highway patrol picked her up in Meruk County, on Highway 9 outside Aspendale. Do you have any idea who she might be?"

"Her name may be Sally Bee, a young woman who's been missing for a few days now. The person to contact is Henry Howling Wolf, her partner." I gave her his number.

"Thank you. You've been a great help, Ms. McCone."

"I'd like to help more. I was planning to leave the city today and return to Meruk County by plane. I'll detour to Santa Rosa first. Will you be at the hospital all day?"

"Yes. Probably until midnight."

"Then I'll see you as soon as I can get there."

5:43 p.m.

Santa Rosa, the Sonoma County seat, used to be a medium-size agricultural town, but as I viewed it from the air I saw it had succumbed to urban sprawl. Shopping centers and residential developments spread out from its central core, freeway cloverleafs abounded. It seemed to be well on the way to recovery from the 2017 and 2019 wildfires that had devastated many of its neighborhoods.

I contacted the tower at Charles M. Schulz–Sonoma County Airport, named after the famed cartoonist who'd made his home in the area, and got into the landing pattern behind a Southwest commuter flight.

6:50 p.m.

Alicia Jordan met me at the front desk of Santa Rosa Memorial Hospital, in a large modern complex near the city center. She was about my age, slender, keen eyed, with shoulder-length black hair and high cheekbones.

"I'm so glad you could come, Ms. McCone," she said. "I got in touch with Mr. Howling Wolf and he confirmed from my description of the patient that she is Sally Bee. He was very upset, naturally. He's on the way here, but it's a long drive, and he won't be here until late tonight."

"How is she today?"

"Better, more lucid." Alicia sighed. "We can treat the physical damage, as severe as it is, but I can't get a handle on how to reach her emotionally."

"It might be best if you didn't tell me too much more until I've seen her."

"Right. First impressions and so forth."

During a wait for an elevator and then the ride upstairs, Alicia told me she had been born in Meruk County fifty years ago but raised in Santa Rosa, and that she had watched her surroundings turn into a wine-and-tourism attraction. "There're *Peanuts* statues all over downtown—some of them are pretty ugly. Charles Schulz was a great cartoonist, but people give short shrift to our other outstanding citizen, Luther Burbank."

I learned from Alicia that Burbank was a famed horticulturist and botanist who created more than eight hundred varieties of plants. His home and gardens in downtown Santa Rosa had been turned into a public park that, Alicia said, drew visitors from the world over.

"In spite of those guys," Alicia said, referring to Schulz and Burbank, "Santa Rosa used to be kind of a nothing place. As teenagers, we were always hopping buses to San Francisco, planning our escape. Later on, everybody who could swing it got a job down there. Now everybody's flocking up here. We've got world-class entertainment and restaurants; real estate prices are stratospheric. My ex-husband and I bought our first house for two hundred thousand dollars; it would probably sell for close to a million today. I'm not sure that's progress."

The elevator stopped with a jerk. "Here we are," she said. "Intensive Care is just down the hall."

7:05 p.m.

The head of the woman who lay in the hospital bed before me was thickly bandaged. Cuts and bruises covered Sally Bee's cheeks; her lips were swollen; her left arm was in a sling, her right eye covered by a bandage. Her breathing was labored. Various tubes snaked from her body, and monitors beeped regularly.

I couldn't take my eyes off her. How had she survived what was obviously a severe beating, perhaps torture?

There was a time, not long ago, when I'd been in a badly traumatized state. Shot in the head, unable to move or speak, but fully aware of what was going on around me. They call it "locked-in syndrome," and that's the perfect label. I was cut off even from those I loved most. Sometimes a visitor would touch me, speak to me as if I were a whole person, but because of my lack of response they couldn't know how much it meant to me.

On impulse I reached out and gently touched the young woman's arm. She didn't move, but I left my fingers on her ravaged flesh just the same. In rehab I'd learned about the hierarchy of human needs: first for safety; second for shelter, water, and food; third for love. The needs vary in their complexity from person to person, of course, but the basics remain the same. This woman possessed the first two requirements. I hoped that somehow my touch would communicate a compassionate presence.

After several seconds she swallowed, coughed, and

moaned. When I stroked her arm, her eyelids fluttered and then opened. Her eyes were dark brown like mine, their whites laced with red. She looked at me, unfocused at first, then with what seemed to be some clarity.

"...Hurt me..."

I leaned forward. "Who did?"

She struggled to speak. I waited, still stroking her arm.

"Hurt...kill..."

"Take your time, Sally. You're safe now."

"...So long..."

"Yes?"

"...Want..."

"What? Who?"

"...Henry, please..."

That was all. Her eyelids fluttered shut again. Alicia moved forward, motioned me away from the bed.

7:35 p.m.

Alicia and I sat at a table in the hospital's café. I was hungry, not having eaten all day, and opted for an early dinner of a grilled cheese sandwich and iced tea; she was drinking coffee. Alicia had told me that she cautioned her patients not to drink too much caffeine, but she couldn't make it through the day without it. "This doctor doesn't follow her own orders," she'd added. "She needs to stay awake."

After a moment Alicia asked, "Are you flying back to Aspendale tonight?"

"I could, but I'm not sure what good it would do. Maybe I'll stay down here for the night. Sally may be more responsive tomorrow, and I want to talk to Henry Howling Wolf."

"Do you have a place to stay?"

"Not yet. I'll check into a motel near the airport."

"You're welcome to stay at my place instead. It would be more comfortable."

"I couldn't impose—"

"Nonsense. I'm doing a double shift tonight, filling in for a friend who's on his honeymoon. I've got a fully made-up guest room in my condo, and a little cat named Fuzz who would love your company."

The kindness of a relative stranger.

8:15 p.m.

I took a cab to Alicia's condo. It was in a development near the hospital called the Pines. Eight pale-gray two-story buildings of two units each sat in a U shape around a pool flanked by rhododendrons. The plants weren't flowering yet, but I imagined that when they did, the garden would be spectacular. Inside, her place was spacious and furnished in a style I think of as comfortable modern—deep upholstered chairs and a sofa, ottomans, glass-topped tables towering with stacks of books and magazines. I found the guest bedroom; I'd once lived in an apartment smaller than it.

The little cat that Alicia had mentioned didn't appear until I'd settled myself on the sofa with my laptop. Fuzz was black and white and approached tentatively. I made a clicking sound with my tongue that always calms cats. She cocked her head, then sat down and proceeded to clean her nether regions.

Cats have no shame.

Although, compared to some humans...

There was a message on my cell from Hy: he would be arriving home tomorrow, probably late. I left my own message about where I was, then settled down. In the middle of the night Fuzz curled up and warmed me.

FRIDAY, JANUARY 11

9:10 a.m.

Alicia had come in late, no doubt exhausted, and was still asleep when I got up. I wrote her a note, thanking her for her hospitality, then called for a cab to take me to Santa Rosa Memorial. Once there, I asked at the main desk if I could see Sally Bee. No, not for a while; she was undergoing tests.

I wondered if Henry Howling Wolf had arrived, and I asked the receptionist if Sally Bee had had any other visitors. The answer was yes, but the receptionist didn't know if Henry was still on the premises. I looked for him, didn't find him, then repaired to the cafeteria and treated myself to a chili dog for breakfast.

My eating habits have always been questionable, according to other people. Vegans and some vegetarians consider them disgusting, while "half-assed vegetarians," as one of my friends describes herself, reassure me that everybody slips up sometimes. But even people who sometimes slip up tend to look askance at a chili dog this early in the morning. Hey, though, you gotta eat, and you ought to be able to eat what you want when you want it.

Besides, why would a hospital cafeteria offer chili dogs in the morning if it weren't okay?

I looked at two nurses at the next table who were giving me disapproving glances and winked.

10:10 a.m.

When I came out of the cafeteria and passed through the lobby, I spotted Henry Howling Wolf slumped in one of the chairs. He must have had a long, hard drive down from Meruk County; he was red eyed and disheveled, his hair sticking up in unruly points. He remembered me right away and was surprised to see me.

"What are you doing here?" he asked.

"I came because I'm concerned about Sally."

"Why? How did you know where to find her?"

"From the ER doctor, Alicia Jordan." He looked so distraught that, after swearing him to secrecy, I told him about my true occupation and the job I'd been hired to do.

"My God," he said, "do you think Sally's attacker had something to do with those awful murders?"

"Possibly. But the crimes are different. Dierdra Two Shoes and Sam Runs Close weren't drugged, and Sally is still alive. Have you seen her yet?"

"For a few minutes a while ago."

"How is she today?"

"She's conscious, and her thought processes are good, but God, what those bastards did to her..."

There was relief and sadness in his voice, but anger overrode the other emotions.

"Was she able to tell you what happened to her?"

"Not in any detail yet. Just that she was kidnapped, then taken somewhere, drugged, abused, and held prisoner."

"Kidnapped where, did she say?"

"In the woods near the old monastery."

"Where I found her feather medallion."

"Yes. Do you still have it?"

"No. It was forcibly taken from me three nights ago."

"By who?"

"I don't know, just that it was a man. Fairly strong."

"Why would he want the pendant?"

"No idea—yet."

Henry's hands curled into fists. "If I knew who did all those terrible things to Sally . . ."

"What would you do?"

"I don't know. I'm not a violent man, but they can't get away with it. I don't trust the sheriff, Noah Arneson, to find out. He's a horse's ass. I wouldn't be surprised if he's involved in what happened to Sally and the two murdered women."

"Do you have any reason to believe he is?"

"No. It's not only that I don't trust him. He's a racist."

"Can you think of anyone else who might be involved?"

"I wish I did. But no." He added bitterly, "Meruk County is full of Native haters."

11:45 a.m.

Henry went for coffee, and I read tattered old magazines until he and I were allowed to visit Sally Bee. She was sitting up in bed when we entered the ICU. Today there was a light in her unbandaged eye that brightened when she saw Henry. He kissed her cheek, then sat down beside her and held her hand.

"How are you feeling?" I asked her.

"I'm not sure. You were here yesterday with the doctor, but I don't know you…"

I explained, giving her my real name and occupation as I had to Henry, then asked, "Do you feel up to talking to me?"

She glanced at Henry, who nodded. "All right."

"I'd like to tape our conversation, if that's okay with you."

"No problem."

I got the recorder rolling, and Sally began to speak haltingly. Her voice was hoarse, and she had to stop for breath every so often, but her memory seemed clear. "I went to Saint Germaine to finish a series of pictures I'm hoping to sell to a little historical journal. The light…I couldn't get it right. It was one of those gray days, and the place felt kind of…creepy."

"Were you aware that anyone else was there?"

"Well, I kept thinking I heard noises…noises in the brush, but I couldn't see anybody. Not even an animal. But I remember…I felt threatened. I took my pictures and got out of there and ran down the trail real quick. Then I tripped and fell. After that, I don't remember anything until I woke up in a...an awful place."

"What kind of place, Sally?"

"It was...dark and smelled like mildew. I was lying on a rickety cot, tied up with a cloth over my eyes so I couldn't see. Spiderwebs kept touching my face. Really creepy, like in an old-time horror movie. But it wasn't in a movie, it was real." She started coughing, leaned back against the raised bed. I handed her a cup of water.

I waited a bit, then asked, "What happened next?"

She shuddered. "This big guy, he laid me down on the floor. It was filthy. Mouse droppings, and God knows what other things. He forced me to drink some terrible-tasting dark liquor, poured it down my throat and made me swallow. I blacked out again. When I came to, I was alone. I knew he'd raped me. I was bleeding—he'd been that vicious. He'd covered me with some blankets and left."

"I'm so sorry. Please go on."

Long silence. Then, "I passed out again. Then he and another guy arrived and raped me over and over. I lost track of time. It might've been two days or two years. Everything was muddled. Except for the pain. The pain...!" She began to cry, rasping, heart-rending sobs.

Behind me the ICU nurse's voice said, "I think that's enough for now. Miss Bee needs to rest."

But Sally held up her free hand. "No, I want to finish telling this." She took several deep breaths, regaining control.

"What can you tell me about the men?" I asked.

"Only that one was heavy, one was thinner. They never took the blindfold off, so I couldn't see their faces."

"Was there anything distinctive about their voices?"

"They didn't talk much. When they did, they sounded white."

"Do you have any idea where this place was?"

She shook her head, wiping tears from her eyes.

"Were you conscious when they took you away?"

"Yes. More or less."

"Try to remember. What did you hear? Smell?"

Another long silence, then: "It was cold, very cold. The air...like in the mountains."

"Cars? Anyone else around?"

"No. Just the wind in the trees. Pines. And eucalyptus. I could smell them before they put me in the back of a car."

"How long before they let you out?"

"I don't remember. I think I passed out while they were driving. And they didn't let me out, they dumped me by the side of the road. Like I was a piece of garbage." A fierce anger blazed in her eyes, and she squeezed Henry's hand so tightly her knuckles were white. "I hope I've helped. I want those bastards caught! I want them to suffer for what they did to me and those other women!"

3:27 p.m.

Henry went out into the hall with me for a brief consultation before I left. "'Those other women,'" he said. "Does that mean she knows the men who assaulted her committed the other crimes as well?"

"I doubt it."

"Me too." Then, almost plaintively, "You're going to keep on investigating, aren't you?"

"Yes. I want to now more than ever."

"Because of Sally? Because you're Native?"

"Both. And because I don't like to give up on anything once I start."

"When are you going back to Meruk County?"

"Right away."

"I'll be here until Sally's well enough to go home. You'll let me know if you find out anything?"

"Yes. I certainly will."

7:55 p.m.

My flight to Meruk was uneventful, although thick, dark clouds warned that there might be more snow on the way. A black January night closed in as I landed.

I went straight to Jake Blue's house. The streets were icy, mostly empty, with only a few lights showing. It was like walking through a ghost town.

"I'm glad to see you," Jake said, ushering me in and indicating a chair across from the sofa. "Where have you been?"

"San Francisco. I had business there."

"Something happened while you were gone. Sasha Whitehorse has disappeared."

"Sasha—the woman who works at Good Price? When?"

"Last night, I guess. She left the store at the end of her shift with some plastic flowers she'd bought to decorate her parents' graves. The flowers were there this morning, and there was evidence something—or someone—had been dragged down the slope to the gate. Nobody's seen her since."

"What do the authorities say?"

"The *authorities*? You mean Arneson? He won't do any more to try to locate her than he did with the others."

"You're sure of that?"

"Sasha's Native, isn't she?" After a pause, he said, "Dammit, she's such a nice girl. Had aspirations, wanted to get out of here, maybe go to college."

Although I already knew his history, I asked, "Did you go to college, Jake?"

"Cal Poly at San Luis. But I only stayed two semesters. I didn't fit in down there, I wasn't smart enough. And then Josie died, so I came back here."

"You were badly hurt by her death. Badly enough to see a doctor?"

"Doctor? You mean a shrink? Hell no. There isn't one that I know of in Meruk County, and even if there was, I wouldn't have. I don't believe in that stuff. Just a waste of time and money."

"What about medication?"

"You mean drugs?"

"Antidepressants, that kind of thing."

Jake wasn't buying my offhand attitude. He stared at me. Then he went to the kitchen, and I heard the freezer door open. When he came back, his hands were balled into fists.

He said, "You prowled around when you were

alone here, didn't you? The vial of that liquid is missing—you found it and took it. Why?" His face darkened with anger.

There was no point in denying it. I'd been leading up to confronting him about it anyway. I said, "There's something I've been meaning to tell you."

"And what is that?"

I told him my occupation, explained briefly about my investigation.

"So that's it," he said when I finished. "I figured you for somebody other than you said. But I didn't imagine you were a private investigator. What did you do with the vial?"

"I had it analyzed in San Francisco."

"And?"

"It's called Arbritazone. A powerful antipsychotic, sometimes used recreationally."

"Well, I don't take the stuff. Not any kind of drug. It's not mine."

"No? Then why did you have it?"

He shook his head. "You must've noticed there's no doctor's or patient's name on the label."

"I did. I thought maybe for privacy's sake—"

"Exactly what I thought. But that doesn't matter. It's evidence."

"Of what?"

He was silent.

"Jake, where did you get it?"

"...I found it beside Sam Runs Close's body."

"Next to her? Not in her hand or in a pocket?"

"No," he said. "It was lying there in the snow."

"So it may not have belonged to her."

"No. More likely to whoever blew her away."

"And you took it instead of leaving it for the authorities."

"There you go with that authorities thing again! No way I'd bring them in. Sam had taken enough shit from people around here. I didn't want any more of it heaped on her after she was dead."

"She took shit because of her activism?"

"That, and other things."

"Like drug use? Bart Upstream told me she was pretty wild for a time after her brother was killed."

He didn't say anything.

"Would Sam have taken Arbritazone?"

"I doubt it. She experimented in her wild phase, but she was, I don't know, selective. She knew what certain drugs can do to you."

"Do you have any idea of who around here might be into that kind of drug?"

"No. I wish I did."

It was almost nine o'clock, I realized. I told Jake it was time I got back to where I was staying.

"Walking around at night's not safe, you ought to know that by now. Why don't you stay here? The couch opens into a bed, and I'll loan you a robe and give you first dibs on the bathroom."

The idea appealed to me: a warm fire and a soft bed versus hiking through the rugged forestland. Still, I couldn't accept his invitation. No matter how angry and bitter he seemed about Josie's death, or how he'd explained about finding the Arbritazone, I still couldn't dismiss him as a suspect.

"No," I said, "I'd better go."

9:09 p.m.

The branches of the trees in the forest whipped around in sudden blasts of icy wind. Although I had my flashlight, patches of black ice made my footing treacherous.

I saw no one, heard nothing, yet I had a vague, prickly feeling that I wasn't alone in the woods, as if someone might be following me. Jake? I doubted it; he'd seemed to respect my privacy. No one besides him and Hal Bascomb could know I was back in the area—yet the feeling persisted. I kept my hand on the butt of the .38 deep in the pocket of my parka and walked faster.

The shack loomed ahead, silhouetted against the moonlit sky. It didn't look as though anyone had been prowling around while I was away. I stopped as I neared it, listening. Nothing but the wind. Just nerves, I thought, because of the previous attack.

The pathway was slick; I eased along, fumbled with the chains and padlocks, let myself inside, and locked the door. The air was frigid; I could see my breath. I kicked off my boots, climbed into the sleeping bag with all my clothes on, and pulled the extra blankets over it.

I couldn't get to sleep right away; thoughts of the shooting incident at the agency, Sally Bee's traumatic experience, and Sasha Whitehorse's disappearance kept cycling in my mind.

I tossed around, put the pillow over my face. Dozed for a bit, then turned on my side and dislodged the pillow onto the floor. My foot was bent in an awkward position. When I shifted, my arm became trapped in the sleeping bag's lining. I got up, retrieved the pillow, and climbed back into the bag. Rearranging myself helped, and in time I drifted off.

11:55 p.m.

I sensed that some time had passed when I was awakened by a howling gust of wind that rattled the shack's walls. I checked my watch, then lay back against the pillows and dozed again.

I woke up almost immediately when my nostrils began to tickle and I started coughing. I wriggled my nose, sneezed. Sat up, still coughing and disoriented.

Smoke. Heat. And a chemical odor.

Disorientation quickly gave way to alarm.

Fire!

The shack was on fire!

I kicked free of the sleeping bag, reached for my parka where it hung on the hook near the door. Struggled into it, the armholes eluding me. When I had it on I ran to the door. The key wasn't in the padlock. What the hell had I done with it? And where were my waterproof documents bag, my gun?

The heat and smoke were stronger now. So was the chemical scent—kerosene. My eyes stung, tears coursed down my cheeks, my nose ran. I could hear the crackle of flames.

I could die in here!

I stumbled back to where I'd left my clothes. The keys were in the back pocket of my jeans; my fingers hooked the chain and pulled them out. Then I located the documents bag, carried it with me to the door. The .38 was still in the pocket of my parka.

My hands were shaking so hard I couldn't hold the hasp and padlock steady. I dropped the keys on the floor, scrabbled around, found them again. I was choking and could barely see, and the fire noise was louder. I got a left-handed grip on the padlock, finally managed to insert the key into the slot and get the staple released. I undid the chain, pushed the door open. Fell out onto the cold ground.

It took a few seconds to scramble to my feet and a few more for my senses to return. The shack's front and side walls and roof were ablaze, giving off waves of heat and kerosene-laden smoke. Wind-driven embers had already set fire to some of the winter-dry aspen trees nearby. Where to go, where to find safety from the conflagration?

The river. The stone bridge.

I staggered away from the shack on the rough, muddy ground. The riverbank here was steep; I tried to run down it, lost my balance, and slid the rest of the way on my ass. The shockingly cold water took my breath away. I went under, then surfaced, choking and gasping. I couldn't get enough air into my lungs.

The swift current pulled me backward, then down again. I came up with a mouthful of water, spit it out. The current still held me, carrying me farther away from the shore. I reached for an overhanging branch, caught it, but then it broke and slipped from my grasp. I went under again. The water was filling my throat, and I couldn't breathe.

I flailed around, working with my arms to resurface.

Finally I broke the surface and got my breath back. My feet touched bottom. I moved clumsily to the far shore, pulled myself half out onto the bank. Rolled onto my side, spitting out water. Across the river I could see the flames shooting skyward from the shack's roof.

I must have passed out then, for how long I don't know. When I came back to awareness, I heard sirens and men shouting. Dark shapes appeared on the far bank, and flashlight beams found me.

The next thing I knew, strong arms had hold of me and were pulling me the rest of the way out of the river. I started choking again. A man's voice said, "Spit it up." He turned me over, clasped me around my middle, and forced me to regurgitate more water. Then someone else took me from him.

Soon I was lying on my back on a stiff surface, and then it was moving. Voices shouted, red and blue lights flashed. I tried to speak. Couldn't. My vision blurred.

Am I going to die?

No, dammit. No, I am not *going to die!*

SATURDAY, JANUARY 12

6:30 a.m.

I was lying on the grass behind my house on Church Street. Naked, and my breath came in short rasps. The house was consumed by flames. The cats? Where were they? Not in there. Please, not in there!

A soothing voice, a cool hand on my forehead. "Just a bad dream. Go back to sleep."

Water down my throat. I feel so heavy.
Can't spit it up. I'm sinking.
Can't move my arms.
Is this what it's like to drown?
Cold...so cold and tired. It would be easy to let go...
Let go, yes, let go...

I struggled to sit up, opened my mouth to scream. The sound that came out was an ugly guttural noise. A gentle hand settled me back on warm pillows.

"It's all right, Ms. McCone. You're safe, you were just dreaming."

Who owned this voice? All I saw at first was blurry white. Then a face emerged: kindly blue eyes, dark hair.

"You were just dreaming," she repeated.

But much of what I'd been dreaming of was *real*.

My former home on Church Street in the city had burned to the ground, torched by a client with a grudge against me. My cats and I had escaped unscathed, but I'd lost almost everything—precious mementoes, furniture, electronic devices, my car, all my clothing.

But that was over, long over.

"Where am I?"

"Aspendale Medical Clinic, Ms. McCone. I'm your nurse, Willa Sharp Eyes."

My head was clearing, my eyes open and focusing now. I saw daylight through parted curtains. Morning?

"Your identification was in the waterproof pouch in your parka as well as a gun, and a registration and a permit for it. They're in our office safe.

"Do you remember what happened to you?" the nurse asked.

I closed my eyes. The smell of smoke, the fire, skidding down the riverbank, the cold water. "I do, except I don't know how I got out of the river."

"A couple of the volunteer firefighters."

"The shack—was it completely destroyed?"

"I'm afraid so. Burned to the ground."

My iPad with the case files, my voice recorder, my cell phone, the clothing and other things I'd brought with me—all gone. Even the clothes and parka I'd thrown on were probably unwearable after immersion in the stream. I couldn't help groaning.

"Are you all right, Ms. McCone?"

My throat hurt, my chest ached, my muscles were stiff, but I was alive. I moved my arms and legs under cool sheets. No real pain.

"All right," I said.

"You're fortunate. Smoke inhalation, but no hypothermia. Do you remember what happened?"

I closed my eyes, tried to concentrate. Images played on my eyelids, but not from the fire at the shack. My former home, the vast out-of-control wildfires that had plagued our state in past years, the weary, smudged faces of the firefighters who had fought bravely, the stunned faces of the people who had lost both their homes and their loved ones. And last night I had almost become a victim myself.

Why? Who had known I was staying in the shack?

The nurse—Willa Sharp Eyes—looked so concerned and caring that I hated to lie to her. "I don't remember anything, except for the flames. Maybe later on..."

She offered a few comforting words and left me alone. I slept for a while, until another nurse came in and woke me in order to take my vital signs. "You're doing well," she said when she was done. "Would you like something to help you rest?"

"No, thank you." I needed to stay awake so I could think.

"Well, if you need anything, just buzz the nurses' station."

10:55 a.m.

I wasn't making much headway with my thinking when the door suddenly jerked open and a scowling figure erupted into the room. In the corridor I heard the nurse say, "Sir, sir, you can't—" before the man pushed the door shut in her face.

He stomped toward my bed. He was stocky, of middle height, clad in a khaki uniform with a big gold star on his breast. He was equipped with all the storm trooper paraphernalia: Sam Browne belt with gun and nightstick, radio mic clipped to his shoulder.

He said, "I'm Sheriff Noah Arneson. And I know who you are—Sharon McCone, a private snoop from San Francisco."

I struggled to find the control that would raise the head of my bed. When I finally did, I had a clearer look at his face: wide, double chinned, and red.

I said tartly, "Private *investigator*, Sheriff."

He ignored the correction. "And I know it was that Sisters bunch that hired you to look into the murders of those Native women. If you've found out anything, you'd better tell me what it is."

"Nothing of any significance."

"You're lying."

"Why would you say that?"

"Somebody deliberately set fire to that shack where you were hiding out. Wanted to shut you up."

"How do you know it was arson?"

"A burned kerosene tin in the rubble is the only evidence I need to prove it." He scowled. "Damned lucky it's winter and the woods are half-frozen, or we'd have had a wildfire on our hands. Fire did enough damage as it is. And all on account of you."

"Well, as I said, I've found out nothing."

"No? Then why would somebody want you dead?"

"I don't know."

"Now, you listen to me, missy. This is a matter for county law enforcement. *We* investigate, not some fancy outside detective. *We* deal with our own crimes."

I pushed myself up higher, fixed him with a steady look. "So far, you don't seem to have done much investigating."

His face flushed more deeply, and he moved toward my bed. "We do what we can, and don't you try to tell me otherwise!"

"I understand you're policing a large area with a small staff. I'd think you'd welcome help—"

"Don't need no help. Not from a woman and not from an—"

He broke off, but not soon enough.

"The victims were women and Natives. Crimes better buried in the cold case files, right?"

"Not right, dammit. You were almost roasted alive in that fire. Somebody doesn't want you poking around in my county. And neither do I."

The door opened, and a tall man dressed in white came in. He said sharply, "Sheriff Arneson, I'm Dr. James Williams. My patient has not been cleared to have visitors, especially ones who barge in unannounced. I suggest you leave."

Arneson's mouth worked, but he bit back whatever reply he'd been about to make, whirled, and left the room.

The doctor closed the door behind him. "Annoying man," he said. "Let me take your vitals, Ms. McCone, and then I'll leave you to rest."

2:02 p.m.

I jerked awake. I'd not only rested, I'd gone back to sleep. But the unpleasant aura of Arneson's visit lingered. I was thirsty, and there was a carafe of water on a stand next to the bed. I poured a glassful and was drinking from it when Willa Sharp Eyes came in. When she saw that I was awake, she said I had a visitor. Did I want to see Allie Foxx?

"Yes, please."

Allie came in, carrying a tote and a garment bag, and stepped close to the bed. She seemed tired, deep circles under her eyes. "You look okay, Sharon, but how do you feel?"

"Well enough to get out of here soon."

"That's what I brought these for." She set the bags down. "New wardrobe, courtesy of the Sisters. A new cell phone too. We figured you must've lost everything in the fire."

"Pretty much, except for my identification and my gun. I was wondering what I'd do for clothing. Thanks, Allie."

She sat in a chair next to the bed. "There's a Jeep waiting for you outside, courtesy of my brother-in-law, who has a dealership in Ames. God, I'm so sorry this happened to you! Do they know yet what started the fire?"

"I think it's more who than what."

"Arson?"

I nodded. "Someone must have found out who I am. Maybe they discovered I was keeping my plane here and looked up the registration. Every plane has an identification number prominently displayed on it, and the number is a matter of public record."

"The murderer?"

"Or somebody else involved."

"So what are you going to do now? You haven't any place to stay. How will that affect your investigation?"

"I'm not sure yet. But it's not going to stop me from pursuing it."

"Where will you stay? Neither of the motels is very comfortable, or very clean."

"And too public in any case. A private home in the village would do," I said, thinking hesitantly of Jake's.

"I know! One of the Sisters, Jane Ramone, lives here in Aspendale. She's very hospitable, and I know she has plenty of room. Shall I call her?"

"Please do."

She began dialing her phone. When she disconnected, she said, "Jane will expect you whenever they release you. She may not be home, but there's a key under the big yellow flowerpot. Three-ten Easy Street—if you can believe such an address."

Easy Street. Just where I've always wanted to live.

2:20 p.m.

I was antsy to get out of the clinic. I rang the nurse's station. Willa Sharp Eyes came in response, and I told her I felt fine, only a slight exaggeration, and was ready to leave. She said she'd check with Dr. Williams, who was with another patient.

Meanwhile I had another visitor: Jake Blue. He looked less than friendly but sounded concerned when he asked how I was.

"I'm okay. Mending."

"You sound kind of hoarse."

"That's what I get for drinking gallons of the river water."

"When I heard there'd been a fire victim, I just knew it was you. I called the clinic and they confirmed it. Somebody found out where you were staying and deliberately set that fire. A friend of mine was out at the scene, a first responder. He said it was arson."

I didn't tell him of Sheriff Arneson's visit, just said, "I figured as much."

"Are you going to keep on with your investigation?"

"Damned right I am. Nobody tries to make toast out of me and gets away with it."

"You have any idea who did it?"

"Whoever murdered Sam Runs Close and Dierdra Two Shoes, probably."

"Yeah, and that could be anybody. This county's full of guys with one agenda—do what they want and take what they want for themselves. Take from the Natives, who owned the land in the first place. From the ordinary people, who've got a right to a decent life here. From uppity women, gays, liberals. Hell, it's the same all across this whole damn country."

"The Harcourts, for instance?"

"Yeah, the Harcourts. Other rich and powerful types like them."

"Such as?"

"The Hellmans. Peter Hellman made his money in Silicon Valley, retired here. He doesn't do anything with his land, but I hear he still runs financial stuff from an office in his big house. Abe Hope—he owns the lumberyard where I work."

"Anyone else?"

"There're all sorts of people scattered around on big pieces of property around here. Nobody knows what they're up to. All sorts of scuzzy types too, who'll do anything for money."

"Like the pair who work for the Harcourts, Gene Byram and Vic Long?"

"Yeah, like them. They've got a hand in dirty jobs all over the county." Jake paused, frowning. "Didn't you tell me you ran into those two?"

"Yes."

"They hassle you?"

"No. What kind of dirty jobs?"

"Debt collecting—there's a lot of gambling in these parts, both legal and illegal, in and out of the casinos. Smacking people around when they get out of line."

Setting a deadly fire if they were ordered to?

I didn't give voice to the thought. Instead I said, "You've lived here nearly your whole life, Jake. What makes this county so valuable to rich people like the Harcourts? Mining? Oil? Natural gas? Other resources?"

"There's never been much of that to exploit. Silver, at one point, but those mines played out early last century."

"And the two women who were killed—what connection is there between them and the powers that be?"

He was silent for a time. "Don't know that either. I understand what you're trying to do. But what happens now? You can't go up against people like the Harcourts and Peter Hellman and Abe Hope unless you've got proof one or more of them's a murderer."

"Finding the necessary proof," I said. "That's what happens now."

5:10 p.m.

Dr. Williams pronounced me fit to leave the clinic. I would have gone anyway, but I was glad to have his okay. I unwrapped the clothes Allie had brought: undies, narrow-legged jeans, a warm sweater, and a fleece-lined jacket. I dressed and went to the admissions desk to check myself out and to pick up the pouch containing my ID and .38 as well as the keys to the vehicle the Sisters had provided. It was a somewhat dinged Jeep Cherokee at least a dozen years old, but it ran and handled well, and the gas tank was full. Before following Allie's directions to Easy Street, I detoured to the airstrip to get the sectional charts from my plane.

Hal was glad to see me up and around. He said, "I called Hy this morning and filled him in on what happened last night, told him you were okay—I'd called the clinic earlier to verify that. He wanted to fly up here, but I discouraged him."

"That's good; he's got enough on his plate, given the shooting at our agency."

"If you don't mind my asking, do the two of you ever get to spend any time together?"

"Not as much as we'd like."

"But when you do...?"

"It's terrific. Hal, did anybody come around the airstrip inquiring about my plane?"

"Sure did," he said. "Paul Harcourt. I claimed I didn't know you or the plane, and all the time it was sitting safe and sound in that little hangar. Us guys who stray a little to either side of FAA regs got to stick together."

"Could he have snuck a look inside the hangar?"

"I suppose he could have."

And gotten the registration number if he did, which would give him access to all sorts of information.

"By the way," Hal said, "there's been a good deal of air movement up at the Harcourt ranch the past couple of days. Planes coming and going. Must be a big conference of some sort."

"Any idea where the planes are coming from?"

"At least one from out of state that I saw."

"Interesting. Keep on top of it, please."

"Happy to do so."

6:01 p.m.

Jane Ramone's house was a white A-frame of the type that had been popular in the 1970s. A row of eucalyptus sheltered it from the prevailing winds. As I approached the door, a series of yips told me that I was about to encounter a very formidable canine.

"Shut up, Cassie," a voice inside said.

The woman who opened the door was short, with unruly dark-brown curls, and was clad in a purple floor-length dress. In her arms she held a wriggling ball of blond fur.

"Hey, Cassie," I said.

The dog stopped wriggling, and its black shoe-button eyes stared at me.

I patted its head. "Friends?"

"Yip!" Cassie licked my hand.

"Friends," I said.

"Yip!"

The woman, Jane Ramone, set the dog down. "Good to meet you, Ms. McCone. I see you're a dog person."

"An animal person—all kinds."

"Are you hungry, thirsty?"

"Famished and dry."

"Come this way."

She led me down a long hallway where the walls were hung with intricately woven tapestries.

"Yours?" I asked.

"My favorites, yes. The ones I can't bear to part with. I'm a weaver, have a shop in town, but I keep myself poor by being unable to part with the work I like. Sit down. I'll be back in just a minute."

While I waited, I called Hy on the new cell Allie had brought, and he answered immediately. "McCone, I was hoping you'd call," he said. His voice was strong, steady, and it braced me.

"Are you back in the city?"

"Yes. At the agency assessing the damage. Hal told me about the fire up there. Sure you're okay?"

"Good as new. But it was pretty scary. I kept thinking of when my house on Church Street burned."

"You're lucky you got out in time. Listen, maybe you'd better give up on this case before there's another attack on you. It should be in the hands of the feds anyway."

"Well, it doesn't seem they're interested. At least, I haven't seen any three-piece-suiters pussyfooting around here. Only the sheriff, and he's too fat to pussyfoot."

"Why haven't the feds been called in about the fire? It was on Native land."

"But not reservation land. There's a difference. Anyway, I'm not giving up. I'm making some headway, but another woman's gone missing."

"You want me to come up there and give you a hand?"

I did and I didn't. "You've got the reconstruction at the agency and the investigation into the shooter's motive to contend with. I can handle things here. And I'll be extra careful."

Long pause. "Okay. But I'm going to put in a call to Ike Blessing at the FBI, have him contact you on your cell."

"Service is spotty up here. He can also try me at the place where I'm staying now." I gave him Jane's number.

"Jesus, where are you? The end of the earth?"

"You remember what it was like when I first started going over to see you at your ranch in Mono County?"

"That bad, huh?"

"That bad."

Jane returned after we ended the conversation, carrying a platter of little sandwiches, a bottle of wine, and two glasses. "Meruk's finest," she said as she poured.

I tried not to gobble, but it was impossible. Jane smiled benevolently and stirred the logs in the fireplace.

"So you're here about our poor lost ladies—my terminology," she said.

"Yes. The Sisters hired me."

"Allie Foxx told me. They're good people, and Allie's an effective leader. I got my degree in political science from Sacramento State, worked in government down there for as long as I could stand it. When I came back here—after divorcing my obnoxious lobbyist husband—the Sisters took me in, made me a part of their group."

"Have you lived in Aspendale long?"

"Fifteen years, ever since I came back to the county."

"What can you tell me about people in the village, whites and Native Americans both? Jake Blue, for example."

"We're all people, aren't we? About Jake..."

She hesitated. "Jake can be...problematical. He's an angry man, but also curiously passive. I've known him my whole life, but I've never been able to get a grasp on what motivates him."

"His sister's murder—"

She shook her head. "More to it than that. Have you had any dealings with him?"

"Yes, and I share your feelings about him. What can you tell me about the missing girl, Sasha White-horse?"

"A lovely child. I pray she hasn't been harmed. She's smart, graduated at the top of her class. Her home life was bad—mother abandoned the family when Sasha was a baby, father's a drunk. Sasha holds things together, works hard, wants to get out of here. But lately she's gotten involved with the folks at Hogwash Farm, is living with some boy out there."

"Hogwash Farm? What's that?"

"An old farm on Roblar Road east of town. The man who owns it lets a group of unemployed young people live in his barn in exchange for doing chores."

"What sort of young people?"

"A mixed group of Natives and whites. Some of them—Sasha included—are conscientious. Others drop in for brief periods, do nothing, and leave. I understand this is typical for these communes."

"It's a pattern that's existed for at least fifty years—more, maybe."

"Well, with one or two exceptions, the young folks at Hogwash are foolish and won't last out one of our winters."

"I thought this *was* winter."

"Oh, you haven't seen anything yet. Come February..."

I made a mental note to check out Hogwash Farm. "Any other local residents you can tell me about?"

"Well, there's Henry, but you know him. Sally Bee—talented little thing, came up here from the midcoast to do some work, met Henry, and decided to stay. Miz Hattie—she's a nutcase. Harmless, but crazy."

"What's your opinion of the Harcourts?"

"The princes on the hill? I only know them by reputation. They're snooty, wouldn't lower themselves to visit a Native weaver's studio."

I tried to stifle a yawn, but it forced its way out. "Sorry," I said.

"You're exhausted." Jane got up from her chair and led me down the hall to her guest bedroom. "Sleep tight," she said—something I hadn't heard since my mother used to tuck me in as a child.

SUNDAY, JANUARY 13

I sat at Jane's kitchen table poring over a sectional aviation chart for northern California and southern Oregon. Sectionals—an informal term derived from their propensity to fall apart along their fold lines— are fascinating documents. Among other things, they tell you terrain elevations; airports; landmarks such as buildings, lakes, and rivers; navigation routes; and airspace restrictions. Flight computers are standard now, but for those of us who enjoy maps, a sectional is a thing of joy.

I moved my finger along slowly, tracing small ranch roads and larger arteries, noting peaks and valleys. The territory I was interested in showed no restricted areas for military installations, no sensitive areas for nesting birds. Small strips abounded, but the chart showed most were not open to the public, as was the case with the one I was looking for: SupremeCourt, a play on the name Harcourt. Elevation 2,701.

Now I scanned the land around it. There was a high mass marked "Peak" and a lower land rise not far from the strip to the west, elevation 2,902, in a section marked "Ranch." The Harcourt property. The land rise would provide an excellent vantage point for keeping track of what was going on at SupremeCourt, if I could get to it.

A main road—Highway 9, where Sally Bee had been dumped—passed about a mile below the peak. Another road intersected with the highway and meandered up to the high mass; in between was open, hilly land. The highway was at 1,912 feet. Could I climb up across the area between the road and the peak lugging the equipment I needed to take? I doubted it.

I called Jane at her shop and described what I was looking at.

"Your map doesn't accurately reflect the other side of Sheik's Peak," she said. "There're hiking trails, but you have to know the territory to find them. We used to hike all around there when we were kids."

"Sheik's Peak. Odd name."

"It's been called that for a century or more. Nobody around here seems to know why."

"Do any of the trails extend onto the Harcourt property?"

"I'm not sure, but that's posted land if so. No trespassing."

"Who would know for sure?"

"Jake Blue. Nobody knows that country better than Jake."

9:02 a.m.

I continued to study the sectional, then finally picked up my felt-tip and drew a circle around the land rise overlooking the Harcourts' airstrip, some two hundred feet higher and two miles away.

My next move, I decided, was to make a reconnaissance flight over the Harcourts' property and airstrip. I drove to the airport, and within an hour I was airborne in my Cessna, through a light fog that dissipated as I gained altitude.

Aspendale looked tidy from high above, buildings arranged on a grid that ended abruptly at flat, winter-brown pasture where cows grazed. I spotted part of the silvery Little White River snaking through forest-land to the east, and to the north the rugged peaks of the Meruk Range, jutting up dark and threatening. There was a reservoir, its ripples winking in the pale sunlight, and beyond it a flat bluff and the buildings of the Harcourt cattle ranch.

I made a descending turn and flew toward the bluff.

The main ranch house was a sprawling white stucco structure with satellite dishes on the roof. There were galvanized iron barns and outbuildings and a hangar at the airstrip, all the roofs painted rust red. The airstrip had a well-paved runway—9/27—taxiways, gas pumps, and a small terminal. A few single-engine planes and one small jet were tied down near the terminal. There were no people out and about in the area that I could see.

I picked up my microphone and tried to get through to a UNICOM. Nothing. Why not, with all the other conveniences?

Jake Blue had told me the ranch was maybe forty-five thousand acres; scattered herds of cattle grazed on the long stretches of open pastureland below the bluff, but not as many head as I would've expected. Maybe the cattle were a hobby—or a cover.

I ascended and circled over the land again. Besides cattle graze, some of it was covered in forest, mostly pines. To the north a massive stone formation, some hundreds of feet tall and wide, dominated the high ground, a remainder from when volcanic activity had spewed such masses upward into the deserts. This was Sheik's Peak, as I remembered from my sectional.

1:20 p.m.

When I got back, I asked Hal for directions to Roblar Road and Hogwash Farm. It was a short distance outside Aspendale to the southwest, and I found it easily enough.

The ranch house was clapboard that had long ago turned gray. A dilapidated swing with many of its slats missing rocked on the porch in the faint breeze. I knocked at the door, and after a few moments a series of thumping noises came from within. The door opened with a creak, and an old man with a long white beard looked out at me. His face was sculpted by the wrinkles that come from long exposure to the sun, and his freckled head was entirely bald, as if all of his body's energy had gone into creating the beard. When he spoke his voice was gravelly.

"You must be looking for the kids," he said.

"The kids?"

"Them down at the barn." He gestured to my right.

"Sasha Whitehorse and...?"

"Yeah, them. Sasha and Whitney and Gloria and Daniel. They run the farm for me, and I let them have the barn in exchange."

"Oh, right. Jane Ramone told me about your arrangement. Is that the barn over there?" I pointed to a structure even more dilapidated and graying than the house.

"Nah, that's an old wreck. Where they live is a prefab they put together themselves. What you do is go through those pines and you'll find it in the clearing."

I thanked him and went through the dense trees, batting away branches. The wide space beyond was full of dead weeds flattened by the rain and snow. A bright-red barn sat on its far side, smoke coming from a stovepipe chimney. I braved the weeds, occasionally slipping into the mud beneath them.

A tall, skinny man with long blond hair answered my knock. "Hi," he said, "I'm Whitney." Two other shapes appeared in the dim light behind him. "And this is Daniel and Gloria. Come in."

I wasn't used to just showing up and being asked in—not in my line of work, where my appearance wasn't always greeted cordially. "Did the man at the farmhouse phone you?"

"Right," Whitney replied. "He always alerts us to visitors."

Why was that necessary? I wondered. Probably they were growing dope or cooking meth.

I entered, studying the three people in front of me. Daniel was medium height and stocky, with thick black-rimmed glasses. Gloria was short and overweight, with a cascade of blond curls.

"Have you heard from Sasha?" I asked.

"Not yet," Whitney said, "but she'll show up."

"Which one of you is her boyfriend?"

Whitney silently raised his hand.

I sat down on the oversize pillow he offered me, drawing my legs up like the others. There were no furnishings in the room, except for the cushions and a blue hearth rug in front of the blazing woodstove.

Gloria asked, "Would you like some tea? It's brambleberry, infused with nutmeg. Our special blend."

"Oh, no, thank you. I can't stay long. You don't seem particularly worried about Sasha. Did she say when she'd be back?"

"She doesn't have to," Whitney said, "we're all free to come and go as we please."

"Sounds like a very comfortable way to live."

Daniel smiled. "The world outside—it's too hung up on time. Watches, appointment calendars, date reminders on the computer screen. We left all that when we came here."

"There's not a clock in the house," Gloria said.

"So you have no idea when Sasha left?"

Headshakes. Whitney said, "Our world is come and go. No one keeps track of anyone."

I suddenly felt as if I'd slipped into some time warp to the sixties, to days of freedom and peace and love and—from this vantage point—a fair amount of bullshit.

I asked, "How did Sasha seem before she left?"

"Seem?" Daniel looked surprised.

"As in her emotional and mental state?"

"Oh, that," Gloria said. "She was just like always."

"Not really." Whitney shook his head. "Sasha was worried about something. She's very reserved, and she wouldn't say about what. Besides, when the four of us moved in here, we decided we wouldn't let negative energy invade our home."

"So if something was bothering *you*, you wouldn't mention it?"

"Not if it brought distress to the others."

"Wouldn't the others wonder what it might be?"

He shrugged. "Only if I'd given an indication that I wanted them to ask."

And they wouldn't ask because they don't want to disturb the group's carefully constructed paradise.

I said, "So you don't know when Sasha left, where she went, or when—or if—she'll come back."

"That's about it." Whitney spread his hands.

"Are any of you concerned about her?"

The three exchanged looks. Whitney said, "We wish her well."

I got up and stared at them, taking in their indifference. Finally I said, "What I'd like to know is who programs people like you?"

They looked bewildered.

I left.

3:01 p.m.

It occurred to me on the drive back to the village that one line of inquiry I'd failed to follow up on concerned Dorothy Lagomarsino, Dierdra Two Shoes's mother. The woman had secrets, had hinted to me

that she was blackmailing someone. Whatever it was
had to do with her daughter and was apparently serious enough that one or more of the county's affluent
men were willing to pay for her silence. How to pry
the information out of her?

Take her a bottle.

It was a solution I'd heard voiced in a couple
of movies I'd seen, and, given the accumulation of
Southern Comfort bottles I'd noticed in Dorothy's
home, it was a good one. It had worked in the movies.
Why not in real life?

3:32 p.m.

I wasn't sure what Miss Manners would say about the
appropriate time for getting an old lady drunk, but I
suspected Dorothy got started early. As I approached
her trailer clutching the bottle of Southern Comfort,
I heard strains of music. Perry Como's "For the
Good Times." Dierdra's mother must be in a mellow
mood.

I knocked at the door, and Dorothy called for me
to come in. I entered, holding out the bottle. She
was seated in her lounger, wearing another wildly
patterned muumuu.

"For *me*?" she asked in childlike tones, motioning
at the bottle.

"For you."

She reached for it eagerly, then heaved her bulk
up and hurried to the small kitchen, switching off
the old-fashioned record player on the way. "You

want to share?" she called. The question was voiced reluctantly.

"No, thanks. I'll take a soda if you've got one."

"Pepsi okay? I don't like Coke."

"Pepsi's fine."

I heard her opening the liquor bottle and pouring into a glass. She swallowed deeply, then poured again. On her way past the couch where I'd seated myself, she handed me an unopened can of Pepsi.

"You know how to treat a girl," she said, settling into her lounger. "It's a bribe, isn't it?"

"Right."

She drank and belched loudly. "'Scuse me. I guess you brought me the booze because you want me to tell you about Dierdra and her men."

"Only if you want to."

"Only if you want to," she mocked me. "Why would I do that, and give away the best free ride I've ever had?"

I shrugged, drank some Pepsi.

"I'm not stupid, you know."

"Never thought you were."

"So what'll we talk about?" she asked, snuggling into the chair.

"Dierdra."

"Why? What's the use?" By now Dorothy was getting deep into the Southern Comfort.

"Why not? From what I've heard, she was a good person."

"You know, she *wasn't* a bad girl. She just liked to go out and kick up her heels like her ma."

Leave it to Southern Comfort to bring out her maternal feelings.

"She had a lot of friends, then?"

"Oh, she did—men and women too."

"Who, for instance?"

Dorothy waggled a thick finger at me. "We're not naming names."

"You said 'kick up her heels.' Did she like to dance?"

"That girl would've liked to do nothing *but* dance. And she was good. I was too, in my day. There's this tavern over near Bluefork, called the Other Place, they welcome Natives. The Wolf's Den at the truck stop, that's another. She'd go out to one or the other with her friend Kelley and they'd dance till closing."

Kelley.

"What kind of dances did they like?"

"All kinds, but usually peppy ones. I don't remember what they're called any more. My Dierdra, she could sure shake a leg."

"Anyplace else she and this Kelley liked to go?"

"Well, not the Indian casino. It's no fun. You know, honey, you look like you wouldn't be a half-bad dancer."

"Maybe, in high school. But it's been a long time."

"Oh, honey, you're not that old. Now *I'm* that old, for sure."

She frowned, at the point in her drinking where she was headed for a pity party, so I steered her in another direction. "Nonsense, you look fit and healthy."

"Really? I try to eat right, but I could use more exercise." She smoothed the voluminous muumuu over her heavy body and smiled.

"Exercise is always good."

"I guess. But you know what—I hate it."

"Me too. About those other places Dierdra and Kelley liked to dance, maybe I've been to them."

"I'm sure you have. There's a bar someplace over in Modoc County, I think it's called the Raven. Once they went all the way to Reno. I don't recollect—" She broke into a wide yawn.

I decided I'd better move the conversation along quickly. "Kelley must miss her a whole lot."

"Who?"

"Kelley, her dancing partner. What's her last name?"

She yawned again. "Oh, I don't know. They were only close because they were looking for men, and I guess they found them. Dierdra was like me—one man wasn't enough. I told her, grab yourself one of those rich guys you're seeing, get set up for life. And she'd say, 'No, Momma, I'm not ready to settle down to smiling at the other ladies and pouring tea. They wouldn't accept me anyway.'"

"Who were these other ladies?"

"Huh?" Dorothy shook her head.

"The other ladies who Dierdra thought wouldn't accept her?"

"Oh, snooty bitches. Like Emily Hope. Whoops—she's dead. Don't speak bad of the dead. Emily's dead, you know."

"So are you still in touch with Kelley?"

"Yeah, sometimes. She's still out there kickin' up her heels, I guess."

"You seen her recently?"

"No. She used to come around, bring me some flowers and treats. But she's gone away." Dorothy's eyelids were drooping now. "Far, far away. They's always far, far away when you need 'em."

"Where can I find Kelley?"

"Who?"

"Dierdra's friend. What's her last name?"

"I don't unnerstand."

"Kelley, who liked to go dancing with Dierdra."

But it was Dorothy who was now far, far away. And snoring.

4:22 p.m.

When I got back to Jane's A-frame, there was a note to call Jake in the middle of the kitchen table. He answered immediately.

"Sasha's still missing," he said.

"I know. I just talked to the kids at Hogwash."

"Those idiots didn't even ask around about her or call the law! I finally nagged one of Arneson's deputies to check it out. He went to the graveyard, found the flowers, but no sign of her."

"And what did he do then?"

"Nothing. Another case of 'just a Native' disappearing."

The graveyard was not far from Jane's house, Jake told me, behind the Catholic church. I went there to have a look around. The church was small and so was the cemetery, containing no more than fifty monuments, most of them old and weathered and chipped. I walked slowly along the dirt path, past mournful angels and wooden markers with the names worn off and rusted iron fences enclosing individual plots. The sky was gray with approaching dusk, and the pines swayed in the cold wind. Their odor was sharp and tangy, intermixed with other smells that I couldn't identify.

I found the Whitehorse plot toward the rear, up a small rise, tucked away in perpetual shadow. John and Amelia, no birth or death dates on the small stones. A poor memorial, yet their daughter had cared enough to leave flowers.

They were tulips, garishly pink and waxy, spilled on the ground. There was a receptacle for such offerings, but apparently Sasha hadn't gotten close enough to set them in it. It interested me that the deputy hadn't collected them as evidence. I stepped back and studied the marks in the dirt. There was a wide, shallow rut, as if something had been dragged down the rise. Something or someone? If it had been a human body, the person wasn't very heavy—probably as slight as Sasha.

Had the sheriff's department examined the rut? Taken photos and soil samples? I bet not, given the law's carelessness and disinterest in the plight of Indigenous women.

A sudden, heavy wind rattled through the pines, nearly bending them double. I looked up at the sky: black clouds moving in. Rain clouds. But then they veered off and continued to the south. A respite, I was sure, but maybe only a brief one.

6:40 p.m.

I still hadn't heard from Ike Blessing when Jane
returned. There was nothing to be gained in sitting
around waiting, so I asked her if she might know
Dierdra's dancing friend, Kelley.

"Sure," she said. "Kelley Windsong. She's a dancer,
has a studio here in town and also teaches classes on
the rez."

"I'd like to talk with her, maybe get her to take me
dancing."

"You mean tonight?"

"The sooner the better."

"Let me see if she's free and willing." She got on her
phone and held a short conversation. "No problem.
Kelley will come over here about eight."

8:05 p.m.

Kelley Windsong was tall, with her long black hair
pulled back in a ponytail. She wore a woven parka
that could only have been designed by Jane, who
confirmed that by patting it and saying, "One of
mine."

"So," Kelley said, "you're the famous P.I. who's
been giving Sheriff Arneson fits."

"Maybe not famous, but I certainly hope I'm
giving him fits."

"Good for you. Jane tells me you want to go
dancing. Why?"

"Because Dierdra used to go with you, and it might give me a lead to her killer."

She hesitated. "You think he's somebody she met in the bars?"

"Maybe, maybe not. But somebody out there's got to know something."

"Okay, then. Let's go see what we can find out."

8:22 p.m.

The Wolf's Den's sign proclaimed that it was howling, and even though this was a Sunday night and still early, it was packed with customers. Kelley snagged us a booth and went to the bar for drinks. A DJ played records, most of them way out of date—try "Earth Angel" and "I Fall to Pieces." I watched the people on the tiny dance floor. They were a mixed group of all ages: mostly white, but a fair number of Native, Asian, and Black people too. Meruk County's melting pot.

Kelley returned with our wine, trailed by a woman in a red dress. "This is Jeannie Powell," she said, "an old friend of Dierdra's from high school."

Jeannie Powell looked as if she might be years older than Dierdra had been: her hair was sparse and dry, her face lined with wrinkles of discontent, and she was heavy—no, obese. When I asked her to join us, she refused, saying, "I gotta get back to my old man."

"What can you tell me about Dierdra Two Shoes?" I asked.

"Not much. I mean, we was buddies in high school,

but Dee, she always was the pretty one. Had lots of boys, but grown men too. She told me she was aiming for something big."

"She say what that was?"

"Dee was secretive. I just thought she'd been watching too much on YouTube."

"Anything else?"

"Well, she drank too much—but then her mother does too. She was a good drunk, though. Never told secrets."

"What kind of secrets would she have had?"

Jeannie put her finger to her lips. "Secrets are secrets." She moved away, weaving slightly, to the bar.

I asked Kelley, "You know what that means?"

"Maybe she was talking about Dierdra's scams."

"What kind of scams?"

"Any kind—in person, on the phone, by e-mail. She described some of them to me: she'd call someone from a mailing list and say she was from the IRS and that somebody was trying to steal their Social Security number. They'd give it to her, and then she could get hold of almost any kind of information about them— bank accounts, credit cards, all of it. And there was the one where she'd claim to be a friend of their grandson and needed money to make his bail on a trumped-up charge. Nine times out of ten, they'd wire it to her. A lot of the scams involved elderly people. The scammers think they're too addled and dumb to realize they're being conned."

I thought of Mamie Louise. I doubted she—or a lot of other older people I knew—would have fallen for such scams. Although, she'd seemed too accepting of the Harcourts.

"These lists," I said, "where did Dee get them?"

"The dark web, probably. Almost anything circulates there."

"Did she work with a particular person or group?"

"She might have, but I don't know."

"Could one of the people she scammed have killed her?"

Kelley considered. "I'd say no. Dee said she used a lot of safeguards. Plus she had something else going for her. I wish I knew what it was." She looked up. "Uh-oh. Here comes Robbie, the village idiot."

Robbie was short and pear shaped, with dark hair that stuck up in an unruly cowlick. He leaned on our table, looked at me, and said, "You the P.I. wants to know about the dead girls?"

"I am. You have something to tell me?"

"What's it worth to you?"

"If your information leads to an arrest and conviction, there'll be a reward."

"How much?"

"I can't say at this point."

"Well, I got information." He leaned closer. His breath smelled like garlic.

"Then show me."

He reached into the pocket of his windbreaker, pulled out a green scarf. "Here. This is the killer's. I found it up to the old monastery yesterday."

There had been no green scarf when I'd been up there before. I examined it. "What's your last name, Robbie?"

"Givens."

"So your monogram would be R.G."

"Sure."

"Then this is your scarf." I showed him the letters. "Are you claiming to be the killer?"

Alarmed, he snatched the scarf from me and retreated. "You think you're so smart, don't you?"

No, I think you're stupid.

Kelley said, "Let's get out of here and check out the Other Place."

9:40 p.m.

The Other Place was nearly dead. One of its big front windows had been broken and covered in plywood. Someone in turn had covered the plywood with graffiti.

"The impending demise of another business in Meruk," Kelley said. "You want to go in?"

"Sure, why not?"

We went inside. The bar was small, the dance floor smaller, and the music came from a jukebox: the Outlaws—Kris Kristofferson, Willie Nelson, Waylon Jennings, and Johnny Cash.

The booth we chose had ragged slashes in its leatherette upholstery; the plastic cover on the table was cracked and peeling. A middle-aged waitress who looked as if she wanted to be anywhere but here came to take our order.

Kelley looked around at the handful of other customers, then signaled to a lone man at the bar. He came over and slid into the booth beside her.

"Sharon, this is Jim Grimes. He and I have talked a lot about the murdered women. He called me tonight, just before I left my house, and asked if he could meet you."

Grimes was Indigenous, with intense eyes and dark hair down to his collarbones. He shook my hand with a strong grip across the table.

He said, "When I talked with Kelley earlier, I knew I had to meet you. I've hesitated a long time about speaking up, but after talking with others in the area—Jake Blue, Hal Bascomb, the folks at Hogwash—I decided you ought to know. There's a connection between those murders and a guy I've talked to."

"What kind of connection?"

He flicked a nervous glance at Kelley. She nodded, urging him on.

"The guy is from here, and he runs a church in a town called Allium south of Bluefork. It's called the Church of the Native Apostles. It's not really a church, but a recruitment center. He drags people in off the streets—not always Natives, more like Hispanics—signs them up with a worker's contract, then ships them off to jobs in remote parts of the state."

"And takes his fee out of their wages."

"You got it."

"D'you have any contact information for him?"

"No, but the church is in an old warehouse from back in the days when the railroad still moved through there."

"And this guy's name is...?"

"Carey Foote."

"And how do I get to this church?"

"I'll draw you a map." He scribbled on a paper napkin, held it out to me.

"Thanks," I said, "I'll look into it."

"Is there a reward?"

"If anything comes of it, you bet."

After Grimes left, Kelley asked, "Did that help?"

"I think it may."

"Anyplace else you want to go? We could try the bar at the truck stop, but the woman who owns it runs an illegal poker game in the back room. She's very suspicious that strangers might turn her in, but maybe—"

"I think this tour has given me enough leads; let's call it a night. And thank you."

10:45 p.m.

The information about the Church of the Native Apostles was too seductive to resist. I set off south in the Jeep. The moon was full and cast eerie light upon the barren landscape when it came out from behind wind-driven clouds. I felt as if I were driving across an alien planet, one devoid of all life.

I wasn't familiar with the village of Allium—Latin for onion—but the pungent fragrance of the bulbs in the surrounding fields told me I'd arrived at the right place. There were few lights on in the town and no pedestrians on the street; a cold wind swept litter along the ancient rails. The buildings were mainly old frame, paint flaking off; most of the display windows of the stores on the main street had been smashed and boarded up. Something—probably a door—slapped back and forth. The noise startled me, and I whirled and looked around, then laughed at my jumpiness.

The church was located in a pea-green, falling-down structure near the old train yards. I parked the Jeep in the shelter of a huge juniper tree and walked back to a break in the church's rusted black iron fence. A path of broken stones led up to a weathered wooden door, which was unlocked and opened on rusty hinges. Inside, the place smelled of mildew and other unpleasant things.

I hesitated inside the door, turned my flash on low. The room in front of me was more of a ware-house than a church. A pair of forklifts and three dollies stood beside a roll-up door that looked as if it might lead to a loading dock; crushed cardboard cartons and disposal bins full of wrappings lined the opposite wall.

At the far end of the space, a truck of the type that delivery services use was parked. I waited, listening for any sounds, then moved forward. The truck was brown, but the logos had been painted over—a retired UPS carrier. I climbed up into the cab and searched the side pockets and bins.

No registration papers. Nothing except, stuffed into the space behind the seats, a map of Meruk County. I turned my light onto it; there were felt-tip markings describing the route I'd just taken from Bluefork. Allium was located at the far northeastern side of the state, only miles from the Nevada border.

So the Native Apostles was a bogus church re-cruiting and exploiting cheap labor. The surrounding agricultural acres made it a good place to pick up undocumented workers; most would be afraid of being turned in to the immigration authorities and easy to convince to do what the boss man said.

Suddenly I heard a noise nearby. I ducked down in the cab, waited. The door to the loading dock began rolling up, clanging violently. Heavy footsteps sounded against the concrete floor. Then two voices clashed, one angry and raised above the other.

"You stupid bastard, you left the place unlocked!"

"I said I was sorry."

"Sorry doesn't cut it. Anybody could've walked in here and made off with anything."

"But there's hardly nothing here. The next shipment isn't due—"

"Yeah, yeah, yeah. You and your excuses."

"Look, Carey—"

Carey Foote, leader of the congregation. He didn't sound so holy to me.

"You want this job?" he went on. "You wanna keep on feeding your family?"

"Of course—"

"Then let's get going. I guess nothing's coming through tonight."

"So you dragged me outta bed for *that*?"

"Yeah, yeah, yeah."

Footsteps crossed the floor, and then the loading dock door rolled down. Outside I heard an engine start—a heavy-duty one, probably an ATV or one of those awful Hummers. Then there was silence.

I waited. A gust of wind swept against the closed door, making the metallic panels groan. There were no more sounds of traffic from outside. I waited some more, then crawled out of the van, shone my flash around, and moved about the warehouse, shining the light into corners and checking the labels on the broken-up cartons.

"Firestarter."

The Harcourt company.

I tore one of the labels off, then scanned the labels for what the boxes had contained: cameras, video equipment, computer parts. Things that could easily be hijacked and resold at a large profit.

I'd have to learn more about Firestarter.

MONDAY, JANUARY 14

8:30 a.m.

First thing that morning, I called the county D.A.'s office and left an anonymous tip about the stolen goods in the church in Allium. Then I phoned Hy, who was already at the agency. He said, "I'm with one of the contractors who'll put our offices back in shape. They're going to be terrific. In fact, I've thought of a major alteration that needs to be added to the plans."

Hy has many talents: he's a great pilot, a sharp hostage negotiator, an environmental activist. He speaks seven languages—some of them badly—and is at ease in any social situation. Now, apparently, he'd decided to become a general contractor.

I filled him in on the events of the previous evening. He asked if I'd spoken to Ike Blessing and I said no, I hadn't heard from him yet. He said he'd try to get in touch with Ike again and prod him.

"Do you know anything about this firm called Firestarter?" I asked.

"Not that I recall. Have you asked Mick to look into it?"

"He's not having any luck." A lot of noise started

up in the background. "Sounds like the renovations are going well," I said.

"Great. These offices were seriously out of date. I've come up with a new concept. I'm really stoked about it. The décor is going to be jazzed up; I've got Betsy Kline coming in for a consultation."

Betsy Kline: she'd decorated many mansions for San Francisco's "elite."

"Can we afford her?"

"I cut a deal. She wants me to find her deadbeat ex-husband. Anyway, this place is going to shine."

I thought of my former office at All Souls Legal Cooperative—a cubbyhole under the stairs with barely enough room for my desk and a ratty old armchair. It didn't seem so long ago that I'd squeezed into that office. Computers were rare back then, but we did have a network of red push-button phones with twenty-five-foot cords that frequently tangled up like snakes in a basket. Some co-op members lived in the house, turning their bedrooms into offices for the workday. Potlucks and poker games in the big old-fashioned kitchen were frequent. I'd lived a few blocks away in a studio apartment on Guerrero Street, as I wasn't crazy about too much togetherness.

Those were good times. As Hank was fond of saying when in his cups, "Those were the days, boss. Those were the days."

"Hold on a second," Hy said. "Your nephew wants to talk to you."

Mick said, "More stuff on Arbritazone. It can induce a chronic delusional state, and the aftereffects are long range. If a person is exposed to it, even in a glancing encounter, the drug may prey on the central nervous system for years. One doctor I spoke with says the behavior she's observed in overdoses of Arbritazone resembles that of patients suffering from PTSD."

"Violent behavior?"

"It can be. Depends on the individual and their background. If they'd been in military combat, for instance, they might have flashbacks to that and react accordingly."

"Nasty drug."

"Yeah. Don't mess with anybody up there who uses it."

"I won't."

"Anything more you want me to do?"

"Yes, as a matter of fact. Several things. First, info on a man named Carey Foote, head of the Church of the Native Apostles."

"Where's that located? Meruk County?"

"Yes. In a little town called Allium. I went there last night. It isn't really a church, just a warehouse that seems to be a drop for stolen truckers' shipments. I tipped the county's investigators to it."

"And you want me to...?"

"A lot of the broken-down cartons I saw there were labeled 'Firestarter.' Apparently they'd contained computer and video equipment. See if you can link that with the company."

"It'd be a long shot, given that Firestarter doesn't have an Internet presence. What else?"

"Dig deeper into the background on Dierdra Two Shoes, emphasis on her scams—"

"What kind of scams?"

"According to my source, all sorts—phone, computer, you name it."

"Versatile. Anybody else?"

"Samantha Runs Close, Sally Bee, Josie Blue, Kelley Windsong, and Sasha Whitehorse."

"What exactly are you looking for there?"

"Family history, past and present. Entitlements; you have the information Saskia gave me. Property and financial records."

"That should keep me busy for a while."

"We can talk tonight if you come up with anything."

"Okay. By the way, we've received more information on Evan McCarthy, the guy who shot up our offices. He was involved in Hy's drug-smuggling case in Mexico and, in a twisted way, thought he'd wipe out the evidence by shooting us all."

"Twisted is right." Then I said on impulse, "Before I let you go, I want you to know I'm thinking of doing some restructuring within the agency, giving your job more prominence. Nothing just yet, but eventually."

"...You're not thinking of retiring?"

"As I said, eventually I'll restructure. But you, unless you're content to live a leisurely life on the proceeds of your websites and trust fund, are first in the line of succession."

"You really mean that?"

"Of course. Who else?"

Hy came back on the line, accompanied by the loud whine of a power tool.

"Are you the one using that power tool, Ripinsky? I thought you were contracting the renovations out."

"You know me—I loved working construction when I was in my teens, and somehow I couldn't resist." He shut off the noise temporarily. "Here's what I'm doing: the waiting area will be expanded. The old pale-gray carpet has already been ripped up."

"What about the floors?" The underlying parquet floor had been a casualty of a massive leak in the roof two years before.

"I've got a good craftsman to deal with that. I'd better go make that call to Ike Blessing. The sooner the feds get involved up there, the sooner you'll be back. I miss you."

"I miss you too. Hal asked me if we ever got to spend time together. I think we should do something to remedy the problem."

"A week at Touchstone?"

"Something more exotic."

"A real vacation?"

"Yep."

"I can't wait."

9:20 a.m.

I went for a walk after breakfast. When I passed the town's tiny park, I stopped and went to sit for a little while on one of the benches, watching the winter clouds scud by. My talk with Mick about restructuring the agency had been good, but I felt as if I'd promised away an important piece of my life. And the word "retired" horrified me.

I'd worked all my life, even selling vegetables from our family plot when I was a little girl. It was a huge garden; my parents had planted it in the hole created when a navy jet from nearby NAS Miramar had cracked the sound barrier above and cracked our swimming pool below. We grew carrots, radishes, lettuce, three kinds of tomatoes, zucchini, eggplant, beans, and a few (unsuccessful) stalks of corn. More than even a family the size of ours could eat. So I, a budding entrepreneur, had set up a stand and peddled the excess to busy neighbors heading home after work.

In junior high and high school I'd engaged in a number of enterprises: dog walking, babysitting, pet-sitting. Then people in the neighborhood started to hire me to make sure their homes were secure when they went on vacations. In college, my experience had gotten me a job with a big security firm in San Francisco. After graduation, when I found no jobs available for those with BAs in sociology, I'd transitioned to a small private agency that sponsored me for my license, then to All Souls, and finally gone out on my own. The cases I was working were always foremost on my mind.

If I retired, gave up control of the agency, what would I do? Take up a craft—needlepoint, knitting, crocheting? I'd tried all three and found I was hopelessly inept. Read the complete works of Shakespeare as well as several prolific modern writers? My reading was scattershot; I picked and chose among authors I liked and some days read so much my eyeballs ached, while other days nothing interested me. Sports, such as working out and running? Only more time to set my mind to wandering. Home improvements? We'd made them both in San Francisco and at our coastal house and were content with the results. Travel? Not with the world in the shape it was just now. Volunteer? I periodically did, at a food bank. Teach? Programs in law enforcement and criminal justice had been radically cut back everywhere.

I looked up at the pines that towered over me, their tops seeming to pierce the oncoming darkness. All these years I'd walked San Francisco's streets and alleys, running my surveillances and asking my questions. Visiting people in their homes—from the most palatial mansions to the worst hovels. Engaging in dangerous encounters, including being shot in the head and left to die.

I'd had some other harrowing experiences too: saving my childhood friend Linnea Carraway from being shot by a crazy man; being locked in a derelict house by a criminal intent on killing me; rescuing my young friend Chelle Curley from captivity in a dangerous part of town the year before. They'd made me feel useful—and fully alive.

No, I thought, I wasn't going to retire, or even step back. The city—the state, even—was my territory and my home. So was the agency, and so was my work. I was there to stay.

10:31 a.m.

Back at Jane's house, I called Saskia to see if she'd had any luck with the Federated Tribes Genealogical Society in Washington, D.C. She had, and the information was what I had been hoping for.

"The inheritance rights of the Meruk are passed down the matriarchal line," she said.

"So either of the murder victims might have inherited—or been about to inherit—an allotment."

"Correct. Give me their names and I may be able to find out."

"Samantha Runs Close and Dierdra Two Shoes." I added what I knew about each of them.

"Good. Now I must tell you that I've mentioned your search about the two of them to a couple of the women on the moccasin telegraph—Milly Warren and Kiki Curtis. They're rivals in information-collecting activity and likely to have different sources. Besides, I didn't dare to exclude either of them."

"I like that phrasing—'the information collecting activity.'"

"Well, they prefer the term to 'gossip,' even if that's what they're actually doing."

"I like gossip as well as the next person." I read off the number of my new cell phone.

"Let me know if they give you anything promising," Saskia said.

Ten minutes later, as I was pouring myself another cup of coffee, the phone buzzed. "This is Kiki Curtis," a woman's voice said. It was what they used to call a whiskey voice in old movies. "I've been on the moccasin telegraph all night, and I've got some things to report."

"Ms. Curtis—"

"Kiki, please. I'm honored to be gathering information for you. Saskia has explained what you're interested in, and I have a few tidbits for you. Someone has been going around in northern California counties that border on Oregon trying to buy up Native land."

"Any idea who it is?"

"A company called Firestarter. I don't know any more about them—there's nothing on the Net or the telegraph. But I've also heard rumors of threats and possible coercion."

"From whom?"

"You know the Net—a lot of the postings are anonymous. But I do trust the telegraph. People on it are looking out for their own. If I hear more, I'll be in touch."

4:45 p.m.

The day passed slowly. When the phone buzzed again I thought it might be Ike Blessing, whom I still hadn't heard from, but it wasn't. It was Mick, with a preliminary report and a suggestion.

He still hadn't gotten any information on Firestarter. It didn't have a phone number, much less a website; some sort of shadow corporation, evidently. He hadn't yet found out anything relevant about Carey Foote or the Church of the Native Apostles either. As for Dierdra Two Shoes's scams, the list proved nothing other than the sheer volume and variety of criminal activity on the Internet. He was still wading through the in-depth backgrounds of the people whose names I'd given him, hadn't found anything I didn't know so far.

"I was thinking," he said then. "Could you use some help up there in Meruk?"

I thought about it. "Somebody who could work anonymously, yes. I'm getting too well known. But not you. You're too valuable right where you are."

"What about Hy?"

"I'd just as soon keep him out of this."

"Why?"

"He's busy with the renovations, for one thing. And there's been a lot of environmental activism up here in recent years. It's likely someone would recognize him; after all, he's on the boards of at least three prominent organizations."

"Oh, right." A pause. "Well, how about Rae? I can give you her number if you don't have it memorized."

Of course. Rae Kelleher, my best female friend and a former operative.

Rae had once been my assistant at All Souls Legal Cooperative, and when I left the co-op, she followed me to McCone Investigations. Then she met my former brother-in-law, Ricky Savage, and they'd been together ever since. Now she was the author of several critically acclaimed crime novels, but occasionally she contributed to my investigations. Of course I had her number memorized, and I immediately called it.

"How're things with you?" I asked her.

"So-so. Ricky's down in L.A. at Zenith head-quarters. I think he's getting tired of being a record producer and would like to perform more. Me, I'm bored, now that I've delivered the new manuscript."

"So you're not busy."

"Nope. Why? Need a helping hand?"

"Yes, I do. Are you up for a little undercover work?"

"Sure. Here in the city?"

"No. Meruk County. I could pick you up and fly you here tomorrow."

"Where's Meruk County?"

"North, on the Oregon border. I've been working a case here, but I'm getting to be too well known. You could present yourself as a tourist, maybe find out things I can't."

"Tell me about the case."

I went over the details. "I've got three local contacts there: Jane Ramone, Jake Blue, and Hal Bascomb, the guy who manages the airstrip, whom I'll introduce you to when we get there. Whatever you do, steer clear of the county sheriff, Noah Arneson."

"Bad news, huh?"

"The worst. He hates Natives, women, poor people. And he's probably in the pockets of the local high rollers."

"Sounds interesting. Where should I stay up there?"

"They have a couple of motels, but I hear they're pretty awful."

"As you may well remember, I haven't always lived in the lap of luxury."

No, she hadn't. From a cottage in Santa Maria belonging to a begrudging grandmother who had been awarded her guardianship upon the death of her parents, she'd gone to cramped housing in Berkeley, where she'd struggled to support a perpetual-student husband. When she left him, she carved out a cozy nest in the attic of All Souls. After moving with me to McCone Investigations, she met and married Ricky. Now her life included a huge house in Seacliff, private jets, and luxurious vacations, but she was still Rae—

one of the special people who never forget where they came from.

"We'll iron out the details tomorrow," I said.

"Okay," she said, and then added thoughtfully, "Isn't it strange, how we women sometimes speak in the vernacular of our female forbears?"

"What do you mean?"

"'Iron out.'"

"Never thought about that. I haven't owned an iron for twenty years or more."

"I tossed mine out the day I left Dougie."

"A milestone, however small."

"And at a time when our lives turned an important corner over such a small matter as ironing."

TUESDAY, JANUARY 15

8:01 a.m.

While I was preflighting my plane at the airstrip, I told Hal Bascomb I'd be returning with a passenger. "How are those motels outside of town?" I asked.

"Grungy."

"Is there any other place my friend could stay that wouldn't link her to me? Not Jake's or Jane's—she's an undercover operator."

"Well, there's a woman who takes in boarders in season—Hattie Moran. She's kind of...eccentric but well meaning. And she can be trusted not to gossip."

"Will you call her and ask if she'll take in someone off-season?"

"Yes. I'm sure she'd be happy to. She's a widow living on her husband's Social Security, and I know she could use the cash."

1:55 p.m.

The sky had been mostly clear on my flight to Oakland, but on the trip back, thickening clouds over Goose Lake indicated a storm was brewing. I detoured south and set a northeast course for Meruk County. The turbulence wasn't all that bad, but Rae, never a comfortable flyer, gripped the edges of her seat and looked queasy, her small face white in contrast to her wild red-gold curls.

"There's a barf bag in the pocket behind you," I told her.

"I'll ride it out," she said through clenched teeth.

"I'm sorry. I forgot you don't like to fly."

"I like to fly. I just don't like little planes. They make me feel like I'm riding in the stomach of a hummingbird."

To distract her, I said, "You know, I read something interesting about hummingbirds the other day. They're the only avian species that can fly backward."

"Well, don't *you* fly backward. Forward is fine by me." She clutched the seat tighter.

I made another attempt to distract her. "What's the new book about?"

"About four hundred and six pages."

"Come on, give me an idea."

"Well, there's this woman who's living in Mendocino County, sort of near Touchstone, but higher on the ridge, and militant people from the forest seem to be closing in on her..."

Hal Bascomb was waiting for us outside the largest of the three Quonset huts when we landed. He helped Rae down solicitously and offered her a mint that he claimed was guaranteed to combat air sickness. She accepted it and ate two more during the drive to Miz Hattie's Victorian cottage in Aspendale.

The cottage was pale yellow, with all the filigrees

and architectural frills of that era. And Miz Hattie, even though Hal had described her as eccentric, was a definite surprise. Short—no more than five feet— and fragile looking, she appeared at the door wearing a towering hat covered with plastic fruit on her white curls. She grinned at our startled expressions.

"I take my name seriously," she said, admitting us and brushing away a pair of ginger cats who appeared to sniff out the visitors. "I have a world-class collection of hats, and I change them every six hours on the dot—except when I'm asleep, of course. This one"— she motioned at the arrangement of various plastic fruits on her head—"is one of my favorites. The fruit is very realistic, and there's a comb that I can attach a real pineapple to, just like Chiquita."

"It's wonderful," Rae said.

I agreed that it was.

"Thank you. Come back to the kitchen. We'll have tea and cookies." She turned and bustled down a hallway, past rooms crammed with velvet settees and carved chairs and rosewood side tables.

Rae and I raised eyebrows at one another and smiled.

The tea was jasmine—"My father was stationed in Japan for much of his naval career"—and the cookies were cardamom—"It's good for what ails you." Good for my ailments or not, I ate three and asked her for the recipe.

"Your other hats," Rae said, "what kind are they?"

"Oh, baseball caps—I'm a Giants fan. Berets, because I can pretend I'm in Paris. I'm particularly fond of my red fedora; it has beautiful feathers on the brim."

After a while I tuned out the headgear conversation, and when Miz Hattie offered to show Rae her room, I excused myself and left.

3:10 p.m.

Back in the Jeep, I phoned Henry Howling Wolf's cell, and he answered immediately. He was still in Santa Rosa, but said Sally would be released the next morning. "She's doing well, really well, and I can't wait to get her back home."

"Are you concerned about someone going after her again?"

"No way. I've got a Remington 870 Express and know how to use it. If I have to turn the house into an armed camp, so be it."

"What about Sheriff Arneson?"

"I'm ready to kick his ass if he shows up and hassles us."

"Not such a good idea to attack the county sheriff."

"I'm not worried about that. Most of his department would back me up."

"Sounds like he's riding for a fall."

"He is, if I have anything to say about it."

I shifted topics. "The feather pendant of Sally's that I found and had taken away from me—was there anything special about it? I mean, something that would make it different from the other two you made?"

"No. It—" He broke off, then said, "Well, maybe. It was numbered. Like many other silversmiths, I sign my work, and number them to indicate the order in which they were produced."

"So the one I found must be Sally's."

"I'm positive it was. After her memory improved, she told me the son of a bitch who grabbed her near St. Germaine tore it off."

Was the son of a bitch who'd torn it off me the same man? Or somebody else? Whoever it had been, I still didn't know why.

Or did I?

3:22 p.m.

The Aspendale Civic Building was next to the clinic where I'd been taken after the fire at the shack. I asked the young Native woman at the reception desk in the lobby who the county coroner was, and she told me it was Malcolm Hendley, owner of the Hendley Funeral Parlor. That figured. Often in underfunded rural counties, a local mortician also served as coroner.

The funeral parlor was a white structure that looked like something out of the antebellum South that had been shrunk to fit this small backwater town. I entered and was confronted by the smell of flowers—lilacs, maybe, but the odor seemed artificial. The floors were covered in gray industrial carpet, the walls painted a darker gray. Soft organ music came from loudspeakers mounted near the ceiling.

A man clad in a dark suit emerged from a side door. "May I help you? The services for Mrs. Woods are scheduled to start at four—"

"That's not why I'm here. Are you Mr. Hendley?"

"I am. Malcolm Hendley, at your service." He was younger than I'd imagined, maybe thirty, and had the trim body and economical moves of a runner.

I introduced myself. He knew who I was—news travels quickly in places like Aspendale—and was willing to answer my questions. He led me to a small seating area.

"What is it you wish to know, Ms. McCone?"

"You performed an autopsy on Josie Blue four years ago, is that right?"

"I did, yes. The poor girl died of manual strangulation. Her murderer was never caught."

"And you also handled her burial."

"Of course. A committal service at the Aspendale Cemetery."

"Her brother told me a silver pendant his sister always wore was interred with her. Was it?"

"Unfortunately, no. The deceased wore no pendant when she was brought to me."

"Was it ever found?"

"As far as I know, no, it wasn't."

That was all I needed to know.

5:07 p.m.

Rae called with news. "I'm at the Back Woods Casino," she said. "Those cowboys from the Harcourt Ranch you told me about, Gene and Vic, were here drinking in the bar and only too happy to buy me a couple of beers. I got out of them that they did 'special jobs' as well as ranch work. When I asked what kind, they got sort of reticent. But as the bourbon—in their case—flowed, I said I'd heard about the fire at the shack where you were staying, and I got the impression from the sly way they talked and looked at each other that they might be the ones who set it."

I'd figured as much. And if they had set the fire, it had to have been on orders from one of the Harcourts. The surge of anger I felt started me coughing.

"Shar? Are you okay?"

I cleared my throat. "Yeah. What else did they say?"

"Well, Gene grumbled that they'd been sent on what he called 'a lot of bullshit errands' whenever the Harcourts were expecting 'important visitors' lately."

"Did they know who these visitors are?"

"Didn't seem to. Just important people from out of the area."

"Congregating at the ranch for what reason?"

"Neither of them could or would guess—they don't exactly have inquiring minds. And I didn't want to make them suspicious by pressing too hard. The guests usually arrive by air, although a limo has occasionally been seen in the village."

"I wonder if anybody in the village has actually seen any of these visitors."

"Miz Hattie claims she has, but I'm not sure that's true. Anyway, the cowboys left me at that point. Gene said they might be back later if they didn't decide to stay at the peak tonight, and Vic told him to shut up. What's this about a peak?"

"Sheik's Peak. It's a big rock formation north of town. I gather those two guys go around the countryside camping out when they're banished from the ranch, like they did at the shack."

"Well, it could be they're up to more mischief. I followed them out and heard the fat one say, 'As my sainted Irish grandfather would put it, maybe we should spend some time riding the dolly.' That earned him another 'Shut up' from Vic."

"Odd phrase, 'riding the dolly.' You have any idea what he meant?"

"No."

I didn't either, unless it was a reference to one of the dollies I'd seen at the warehouse in Allium.

I asked Rae, "So what's on your agenda for the rest of the evening?"

"Paul Harcourt. He came in alone a while ago—the cowboys pointed him out to me just before they left. Harcourt's playing blackjack. I'm going to try to get next to him, see what I can find out."

"Be careful. He's dangerous."

"I can be dangerous too, you know."

6:30 p.m.

Jake agreed to meet me at the Brews to talk about the Sheik's Peak area. I didn't tell him my other reason for wanting to see him; I would do that after he gave me the information about the Peak.

He was seated in a booth looking worn out. His eyes were reddened from his rubbing them, and his skin was drawn tight over his cheekbones.

We ordered drinks, and when they came I opened

the sectional I'd brought with me. "Let's look at this map. How do I get to Sheik's Peak?"

"You're not planning to go out there alone? That's pretty rough country."

"Don't worry about that. I'll be careful."

He uncapped a felt-tip and began drawing on a napkin. "You take the main highway north for five miles or so and turn left on Powder Gap Road. There's an old, rusted-out Mobil gas sign that tells you when it's coming up. From there it's about two miles before you see the peak. It stands out because it's on one of the high rises of land out there—big, crumbling granite thing. Some of us used to try to climb it, but as far as I know, no one ever did."

"The road doesn't go all the way to the peak."

"No. It ends in a clearing a quarter mile or so below the base."

"Jane Ramone told me there are hiking trails in the area. Is there one leading out of the clearing?"

"Two. One that leads up to the base of the peak, the other parallels it lower down."

The second was the one I wanted. "How long a hike is it"—I tapped the sectional with my finger—"to this land mass here?"

"A couple of miles. But that's on Harcourt land."

"I know." I tapped another spot. "The building marked here near the base of the peak—what is it?"

"An abandoned cabin built by a crazy miner a long time ago."

Gene and Vic's other camping place.

"Tell me again why you think one of the Harcourts killed your sister."

He sighed, took a deep drink of beer. "She'd been

seen with one of them, walking around by the reservoir. More than once."

"By whom?"

"Several people."

"Did you hear this before or after she died?"

"Both."

According to Josie's former boyfriend, the Berkeley professor, on her return to Meruk County she'd found the love of her life. A Harcourt?

"Could she have been seeing one of them regularly without you knowing it?"

"What do you mean, seeing him?"

"You know what I mean, Jake."

"She had better sense than that." He grimaced. "Or, hell, maybe she didn't. Anyhow, she didn't talk about her love life."

I asked, "What motive would either have had for strangling her?"

"I don't know. They've got a mean streak, a crazy temper. All the Harcourts are crazy."

I said, "All right. Now let's talk about the feather pendant that was stolen from me."

"That pendant! What the hell is so important about it?"

"Henry Howling Wolf made only three of them: one for Josie; one for a friend who'd moved to Portland; one for Sally Bee. You told me Josie was buried with hers. But that was a lie. Malcolm Hendley told me hers was never found."

Jake sagged over his beer, both hands now pressed to his forehead.

"You believed her killer might have taken hers, maybe threw it away in the woods. When you saw me wearing the one I found and I told you where I'd found it, you thought it might be Josie's. You didn't know then that Sally Bee was missing, or that she'd been abducted on the trail to the monastery and the pendant was likely hers. So you followed me back to the shack that night—"

"All right!" He lowered his hands, but his eyes avoided mine. "Yes, I followed you. Yes, I wanted the pendant because I thought it must be Josie's, the only thing left of hers that meant anything to me. Jesus, I'm sorry, Sharon, I'm sorry..."

"Why didn't you confess to me later?"

"I was too ashamed. I didn't want you to hate me after the way I jumped you, knocked you down..."

"I don't hate you. I'm just disappointed in you."

"No more than I am in myself."

"Okay. Where is the pendant now?"

"In my freezer. Under the mac and cheese. I guess I'm not very original about hiding places."

"You know now that it most likely belongs to Sally Bee. You'll have to return it to her when she comes home."

"I will. That's a promise."

He looked totally bereft when I left him, as if he were reliving all his mistakes and losses.

6:50 p.m.

The odd phrase Rae had reported to me—"riding the dolly"—echoed in my mind again as I climbed into the Jeep. It had an unpleasant ring to it, although none of the individual words implied anything terrible.

I thought of the warehouse full of stolen goods in Allium. There had been dollies lined up to move the cartons. But you didn't ride them; you pushed them. Anyhow, what could that have to do with Gene and Vic? Or Sheik's Peak?

Maybe it was an Irish slang term. But for what?

"Riding the dolly."

Dolly. Doll. That was a slang word for woman—

All at once I remembered the Irish friend I'd had in college; in his parlance women were "dollies"—and "riding" was a euphemism for "fucking."

Oh my God!

7:24 p.m.

I set out north on the highway from Bluefork toward Sheik's Peak. When I saw the old Mobil gas sign loom ahead, I slowed and soon turned onto Powder Gap Road. It was paved but potholed, and its condition deteriorated even more as it zigzagged upward onto the long, steep hillside that stretched out below the monolith. Made of rough gray granite, Sheik's Peak towered above its desolate surroundings.

The clearing where the road ended was ringed by pine trees. It was deserted—no sign of Gene and Vic. But the Jeep's headlights picked out a rutted criss-crossing of recent tire tracks. At this elevation there were still patches of snow on the ground, even though it hadn't snowed in several days. The peak jutted up from atop a wide rock formation whose sides were steep and eroding. It had been battered by the elements over thousands of years; there were deep fissures in the granite, filled by ferns and lichen, and broken rocks were scattered across the rising ground above. It was at once a symbol of the effects of eternity and a reminder of how we humans crap up the planet.

I parked and got out into an icy wind that made me wish I had a warmer coat and mittens instead of gloves. I couldn't see the cabin Jake had told me about from here; it must be hidden behind the wooded area off to my left. The beam from Hal's flashlight picked out two hiking trails that led across the damp, rutted grass, one upward into the pines, the other in a lower, northerly direction. I took the upper one, aiming the light just ahead of my feet when I entered the copse of pines.

The trail was tough going. I stumbled over rocks, slipped on the icy pine-needled ground, ducked to avoid branches. Fortunately it wasn't a long trek. The copse soon thinned, the ground leveled into another, smaller clearing, and then I saw the cabin—a dark, rectangular shape huddled against the steep wall of granite in the monolith's shadow.

I made my way to it along a barely discernible extension of the trail. It was in far worse shape than my former hideout, built of weathered logs, its sagging roof topped by a lopsided tin chimney. No lights showed through the gaps between the logs. There was no visible window, just a door hung crookedly in its frame.

The door wasn't locked. I took my .38 from the

plastic pack in my deep pocket, then threw the door open, recoiling from the cold, fetid air as I flashed the light inside.

Just a single room, the floor warped and caked with dirt and rodent droppings. A rough table with two mismatched kitchen chairs and an extinguished oil lamp. A red-and-white cooler on a makeshift counter. A cot—with its covers hanging to the dirt floor. And on it—

"Sasha!"

The young woman I'd met in the Good Price Store lay on her back. Lengths of clothesline bound her at the wrists and ankles. When I said her name, her eyes fluttered open and she cringed like a frightened animal.

"Don't be afraid," I told her, "I've come to help you. I'm going to get you out of here."

She shook her head violently and her eyes moved from side to side, as if looking for a way out. Her face was grayish, her hair matted; she licked dry, cracked lips but didn't speak.

Her eyes met and held mine as I went to the cot. Hers were swollen, bloodshot.

I sat on the edge of the cot and managed to untie the knots in the clothesline. She shivered. All that she wore was a man's ragged red plaid flannel shirt. Once I had her free, I took off the wool-lined coat the Sisters had provided me and placed it around her shoulders.

"They hurt me." Her voice was hoarse from crying out to be released from this place, or from disuse. "They both...hurt me."

Gene and Vic. Goddamn them!

A panicked thought widened her eyes. "What if they come back?"

"They'll regret it if they do before we get out of here. Can you walk?"

"Think so."

I helped her up, supported her with both hands, and led her out of the cabin and down the trail through the trees. Although she'd been badly abused, Sasha was able to walk and didn't stumble or fall. When we reached the clearing below, I belted both of us into the Jeep and drove away from there as fast as I dared.

Sasha slumped against the passenger window, her arms tightly folded across her breasts. She breathed raggedly and coughed a few times, but otherwise was silent.

I said, "Did those two men take you from the cemetery when you were delivering the flowers?"

"Yes. I knew them from town; they'd been giving me the eye, and I'd tried to be polite, but this time they didn't say anything, they just grabbed me... There was nobody else around. They put a cloth over my face before I had a chance to scream, and I guess I passed out."

"Did you smell anything on the cloth?"

"...Yes, something like the chlorine in the community center pool."

Chloroform. The bastards had gone to the cemetery fully equipped.

"And then?"

"When I woke up in that godawful place they were drinking. Really bombed. They...they'd raped me. The pain, it was awful, but I lay still pretending I was still out and praying they wouldn't do it again. After a long time they left. One of them said, 'We'll be back, sweetheart.'"

I was sickened by what she'd gone through. Sickened, and determined that the two would pay. I put my free hand on Sasha's arm, and we rode the rest of the way to Aspendale in silence.

9:55 p.m.

Willa Sharp Eyes, the nurse who had attended me after the fire at the shack, was standing at the admissions desk at the clinic when I brought Sasha in. Immediately she asked who had harmed her. I told her I'd found Sasha near Sheik's Peak and didn't know who was responsible for her condition. If I'd named Gene and Vic, it would have meant reporting the kidnapping and rape, and I didn't want to be detained and questioned by Arneson or his deputies. There'd be time enough later to make sure those two bastards were arrested and charged.

Willa dispensed with the usual protocol of forms and insurance information and took Sasha directly to an examining room. When she came back, she phoned Dr. James Williams at home, and he agreed to come in and attend to the patient.

I checked for voice mail messages when I left the clinic. There were two. One was from Ike Blessing, finally, saying he and his partner would be at the Bluefork airstrip tomorrow. But what time tomorrow? I called the mobile number he'd left and was told Blessing was scheduled on an early-morning flight from Washington, D.C., to SFO, ETA as yet unspecified.

The other message was from Mick. "I've got that last batch of info you wanted about Dierdra Two Shoes and Sam Runs Close," he said when I reached him. "They both had allotments of land up there."

"Did they claim the allotments?"

"No, they were killed before they could. But they must have been aware of them."

"What are the allotments worth?"

"There's no way of telling. There aren't any comps. I mean, it's not like measuring the value of a house on Tel Hill versus one in Visitacion Valley."

"Any indication that either woman was approached about selling?"

"No, but that doesn't mean it didn't happen."

"What about Sally Bee? Did she have an allotment?"

"No riches there."

"Josie Blue?"

"Nope. And I'm fresh out of information."

WEDNESDAY, JANUARY 16

8:25 a.m.

J ane woke me by shaking my shoulder. "Your friend Rae is here and wants to see you. She says it's important."

Yawning, I brushed hair from my face, rubbed sleep grit out of my eyes. "Send her in."

Rae looked perky, as if she'd had a good night's rest. She sat cross-legged on the end of the bed and said without preamble, "That Paul Harcourt is one weird dude."

"So you did get next to him last night."

"As next to him as I ever want to."

"Did he hit on you?"

"Oh yeah. Tried to. Wasn't easy fending him off."

"Is that what you meant by weird?"

"Partly. He's so wildly unpredictable. He ranges from being charming to extremely aggressive. Shouted at the bartender when he didn't bring him a re-fill quickly enough, then left him a ten-dollar tip. Called Meruk County a 'shithole,' then praised it as being a wonderful place to live. Came on to me, then started treating me as if I were his best friend's baby sister. He was all over the map. Some people he knew came in and tried to talk to him, but he didn't show much interest in what they were saying. He didn't eat anything while I was with him, just drank. People who are in an advanced state of hysteria often don't."

"You think the term 'hysteria' characterizes his condition?"

"Volatile reactions? Attention-seeking behavior? Everything out of proportion?"

"Right. And I thought the other brother, Kurt, was the crazy one. He was institutionalized a while back."

"Well, I haven't had the dubious pleasure of meeting Kurt. Maybe his psychotherapy worked."

"Do you think Paul's capable of harming other people?"

"Oh yes. Definitely."

"Harming them seriously, fatally?"

"Shar, I don't have to tell you we're in rough territory up here. Some of these people wouldn't have a second thought before picking up a tire iron, a hammer, or a gun."

"Look, I don't want you going anywhere near the Harcourts again. Or those two cowboy rapists who work for them."

"Rapists?"

I told her about my rescue of Sasha Whitehorse.

"Rough territory, like I said. I guess I'm lucky they didn't try to kidnap me."

"I think they mainly go for Natives. Just stay away from them as long as they're still walking around free."

"You don't have to worry about that. So what're we going to do next?"

"*We?*"

"Sure. That's what I'm here for, isn't it?"

"Yeah, but it's too early for me to strategize. I'll get back to you when I'm thinking more clearly."

9:10 a.m.

Jane had gone to her studio, and I was in the kitchen, rustling up some sourdough for toast, when Kiki of the moccasin telegraph called. I let the message go on the machine, then picked up when I heard the urgency in Kiki's voice. "I'm sorry to phone so early, but I figured this information couldn't wait. There is a rumor—a very substantial rumor—that something big is going to happen in Meruk County today."

"Something involving the tribe here?"

"Yes. Our informants seem charged up about it."

"Do they have any idea what it is?"

"Not specifically. Just rumors of a big gathering at a ranch that has some sort of connection."

"Trouble for the tribe?"

"I don't think so. To me it smells of money."

"Big money?"

"Hey, hon, is there any other kind that gets people charged up?"

"Was the ranch named in the rumors?"

"No. I thought you might know."

"I've got a pretty good idea. Thanks, Kiki."

"Glad to help. I'll let you know if I hear anything more."

Something big... today...
Informants... charged up...
Today...

9:31 a.m.

While eating toast and drinking coffee, I'd been aware
of the droning of airplane engines. More of the same
sounded as I finished dressing. I looked out the
bedroom window, but all I could see was yew tree
branches. I started outside to get a better view, and
the phone rang. For me again. Naturally.

"Big birds are descending from the sky," Hal said,
"a regular flock of them."

"Going where?"

"SupremeCourt."

"What kind?"

"Mostly twin engines, at least one small jet."

"Any of them land at your strip?"

"One, a Beechcraft Baron 58P. The pilot wanted
to refuel, said the Harcourt place would probably run
out of avgas soon. Then they took off again."

"How many passengers?"

"Two. Guy named Michael Stein and his companion."

I knew the name; Michael Stein was a major finan-
cier, into about every profitable venture in the city,
maybe the country.

"Has this happened before?" I asked Hal. "So
many big birds coming in all at once?"

"No, not this many at one time. I'd say the

Harcourts are throwing a party—but judging by the looks on the faces of Stein, his companion, and the pilot, I don't think that's the reason."

"Did you talk with the pilot?"

"Sure I did, while he was refueling. What he told me is interesting. He said the guy with Stein was a goon."

"A *goon*?"

"His word, not mine. As in armed bodyguard. He said the goon never moved a muscle during the flight up from L.A., just sat like a statue while Stein talked on his mobile."

"Did the pilot hear any of the conversation?"

"Just a bunch of business stuff—stock options, dollars per acre, transfers of deeds, tribal rights. Didn't mean much to him, or to me."

But to me it did. "Hal, I've got to go now."

9:44 a.m.

How to confirm what I suspected? I needed evidence. Concrete, in-your-face evidence that would stand up in court and yell, "Hey, look at me!"

Look at me. Well, why not?

I got through to Derek at the agency. Avoiding the usual pleasantries, I said, "You know that night scope that's in the equipment closet? The Whisper 3500?"

"I do."

"Will you contact that air courier firm we use and send it and its carrying case up to Bluefork Airport here in Meruk County?"

"Yeah. When do you need it?"

"Tonight."

"Short notice."

"Tell them there'll be a big bonus for them."

"Will do."

Okay, that was taken care of. Now...

I seemed to be spending half my time on the phone lately. Why stop now? I rang up the district attorney's office in the county seat of Ames and asked for an investigator. A woman named Vivian Song answered. She knew my name and why I'd come to Meruk County, said she would have contacted me by now if another matter hadn't demanded her immediate attention. When I explained what I thought was about to happen at the Harcourt ranch, she said crisply, "I'll come down there and we'll talk in person. I can catch a ride on the D.A.'s chopper and be at the airport there in a couple of hours."

Noon

Vivian Song was a petite woman with short black hair and a face that reflected Southeast Asian heritage. She was comfortably attired in green sweats and a heavy shearling coat that she removed and hung on the coatrack by the woodstove in Hal's office.

"As I told you on the phone," she said, motioning for me to sit in the chair next to her, "our office is aware of the recent Native homicides as well as the other murders and disappearances over the years. The D.A.'s office has been quietly investigating, in cooperation with the state D.A., but there have been certain obstructive elements."

"Such as Sheriff Noah Arneson?"

"Right. He's currently out of the loop, however. After you called me, our office discovered there's been some racial unrest down south in Fleetwood, and he's been sent there to quell it."

"My God, he's one of the worst racists—"

"There's been no unrest. But it will take him a long time to figure that out and return here."

"And then?"

"Warrants are being prepared. It seems we received an anonymous tip that our esteemed sheriff and some of his cohorts have been fencing goods dropped off at a warehouse in Allium by long-haul truckers whose employers aren't too careful with their manifests."

"I believe I discovered that warehouse two nights ago."

"So you were the anonymous tipster. We staked the place out and caught two truckers as they attempted to deliver goods. Why didn't you give your name?"

"My history with law enforcement departments has been complicated."

"So I've heard. Now tell me about this drug Arbritazone."

I explained what I knew about it.

"So the drug is not necessarily benign," Song said.

"It's like a lot of drugs—can be used either for good or bad purposes."

"Is anyone marketing it now, do you know?"

"It was used successfully in trials in China, also Australia. The FDA has started testing what few samples they have."

"But it's currently unavailable in the US?"

"Right."

"And you believe a large supply of it is available in Meruk County."

"Yes. Much of it from land that belonged to the deceased tribal members." I told her of the allotments and my suspicion that they, not hatred of Natives or sex trafficking, were the reason for the murders of Samantha Runs Close and Dierdra Two Shoes.

"That sounds plausible. But how is the raw material being harvested? It can't be lying on the ground for just anybody to pick up."

"In a way it is," I said. "Arbritazone deposits are formed in highly alkaline waters and, if you know what to look for, they can be had by digging through the pebbles in streambeds."

"So people are hunting through rocks for it?"

"I doubt many ordinary people even know what it is. But the powers that be have been trying to buy up land where there are rich deposits."

"The powers that be?"

"The Harcourts and probably others. I don't know exactly who the others are yet, but later I might be able to supply their names."

She looked at me, quiet and thoughtful. "You don't give away much, do you, Ms. McCone?"

"Not unless I'm sure my facts are right."

"Okay, I get it. When will you be sure?"

"Maybe later this afternoon."

Song and I talked a while longer—mainly about the kidnappings and rapes of Sally Bee and Sasha Whitehorse by Gene Byram and Vic Long. She was as outraged as I was and assured me that warrants for the arrests of the two men would be issued as soon as she returned to Ames.

2:31 p.m.

Saskia wasn't home. I left a message, rattled around Jane's house for almost an hour, disturbing Cassie's snoring dog on the braided rug. When my birth mother finally got back to me, I told her, "I'm going to be abrupt."

"Why, Sharon, what a surprise."

"What do you recall about Meruk inheritance rights? You've said they pass down the maternal line."

"Yes."

"What happens if the heir dies intestate?"

"Let me look at the information I printed out." Scrape of a drawer, rustling of paper. "Yes, here it is. If an heir dies without a will or issue, all rights revert to the tribe."

"And the tribe can do anything with them? Sell them to non-Natives?"

"They have the right to sell to family members. If not, the land reverts to the Bureau of Indian Affairs or the Bureau of Land Management."

"You mean Natives don't have the right to their land, even today?"

"Correct."

"Then how are private owners—as I suspect they're doing here—getting hold of them?"

"Corruption is everywhere, my dear. Even in the BIA or BLM."

"Thank you! You may have just fit together the last pieces in my case!"

"I'll wait to hear."

5:32 p.m.

Rae leaned over my shoulder as we huddled over the sectional spread out on Jane's kitchen table. "You sure you want to do this tonight?" she asked.

"Tomorrow might be too late. They've been congregated at the ranch all day."

"But it'll be so dark, and the weather is beginning to look iffy—"

"Darkness is the best cover, besides, I've got my night scope." I patted the Whisper 3500 that had arrived half an hour ago. "That'll let me see the numbers on the planes, which are the best clues to who's there. Maybe I'll even spot somebody I recognize. The presence of certain people will tell me if there's something illegal going on there. Then I can photograph them and notify the authorities."

"What authorities?"

"I've got Vivian Song, the county D.A., on alert. As well as Ike Blessing from the FBI; he'll be arriving here"—I looked at my watch—"as soon as he can."

"Well, you've certainly got things organized."

"It's necessary to this kind of operation."

"You sound like Hy."

"Maybe I'm turning into him."

"Uh-uh. He's still got that edge that makes him go off half-cocked."

"That's one of the reasons why he's not here tonight."

She was silent for a moment, then asked, "So when are you going up there?"

"Pretty quick. I've got to get ready."

"Can I come along? Just to the airstrip, in case you need me?"

"Sure. But only to the airstrip."

I put on black jeans and a heavy sweatshirt. I wore my parka, my .38 in its pocket, sturdy work boots, and the night scope in its sling.

"I can do it," I told Rae calmly—all the time quaking in my boots.

7:17 p.m.

A military chopper hovered over the airstrip. Hal looked out into the darkness and said, "Ah, we're about to be blessed by Blessing from the FBI."

I snorted, only half-amused. Blessing had informed Hal that he'd be arriving and asked that I wait for him.

Blessing was a tall, lean Black man with deep brown skin and closely cropped gray hair. His partner, Bob Graves, was his opposite—short, white, and blond. Hal had reserved the waiting room for us, and, when he offered, Ike gratefully accepted a mug of coffee.

"So you're Ripinsky's hero," Blessing said.

"His *hero*?"

"Bravest woman he ever met."

"He told you that?"

"More than once."

"Maybe you should tell him to tell *me* that."

"Will do. So what do we have here?"

I explained the situation.

He said, "I've got reinforcements coming in, but I still don't have probable cause."

"I can get you that." I uncased and showed him the nightscope, explained what I wanted to do.

He was silent for a moment, sipping his coffee. "I can't authorize that."

"You don't have to. As far as you and I are concerned, you don't know anything about it."

Another long silence. "You'll need to be able to communicate—"

"I have a cell."

"You'll need a more sophisticated device than that. We have one in the chopper." He spoke into his own cell, requested the device be brought to him. "State-of-the-art technology," he said to me, "just push the button and speak slowly. Let me see that scope." He took it from me, sighted through it a few times, and examined it more closely. "High quality. I see it can transmit any photographs you take to a linked device."

"Such as the one you're giving me?"

"Correct. And to the one we'll be using here to keep in contact with you. I'll program it in before you leave."

Now I was getting edgy. The feds were going to cut me loose on a very dangerous mission. I swallowed hard, said, "Then you think this will work?"

"If you're up to it."

"Oh, I am." *I think.*

"You don't need to do this if—"

"No, I do."

He studied me. "Why?"

"I don't want to get into a philosophical discussion right now."

"Something about being Indigenous? And a woman?"

"…Both. And some other things as well."

"Are you sure you want to go up there alone?"

"Yes."

"Bob or I can go with you."

"Wouldn't that be involving you in the very situation you can't authorize?"

He shrugged. "Have it your way, but don't take any unnecessary chances. Your husband would never forgive me."

10:43 p.m.

Thickening storm clouds followed me up Powder Gap Road. I tried not to think about what lay ahead if the clouds should break open while I was hiking through rough country. The wind in the clearing was icy, whipping down from Sheik's Peak and carrying the smell of ozone. I parked the Jeep where I had the night before, pulled the wool cap down snugly over my ears, slung the cased nightscope over my shoulder, and switched on the six-cell flashlight I'd borrowed from Hal.

The hiking trail that led away from the peak was easy enough to follow at first, the footing mostly firm enough for me to move at a fast walk. But when the terrain began to rise, gradually at first and then steeply, the going became harder and I had to slow down. Even though I was warmly dressed, the wind cut through and chilled the sweat from the long uphill climb.

I must have gone at least a mile when I came to a fence that marked the boundary of the Harcourt ranch. The trail turned abruptly there, paralleling the fence straight uphill on this side; there was no trail on the other side, just barren land littered with outcroppings and small boulders.

The fence was of rusted barbed wire, but it sagged enough in one spot that I could get over it without cutting myself or tearing my clothing. I set out carefully over the rocky ground. After a short distance it rose sharply into the landmass I'd noted on the sectional. As I climbed I could see below the faint glow of lights from Aspendale and brighter ones from the SupremeCourt buildings.

The ascent grew steeper and steeper. I was breathing heavily, and the muscles in my legs ached by the time I neared a long, flattish section overhung by a sheer rock wall—a kind of ledge that would be the ideal viewing spot. The wind was fierce up here; faint rumbles of thunder sounded in the distance, then lightning crackled.

The ground crumbled underfoot as I struggled toward the ledge. I had to lean forward and dig my gloved fingers into the stony earth in order to maintain my balance.

I was almost to the ledge when the rain started.

It was a light, stinging rain, but I was afraid that it would turn into a downpour and send me tumbling down the hillside. I heaved myself upward, clawing for handholds on the sloping, broken granite side of the ledge. Found one, then another. Managed to haul myself up gasping onto the flattish surface.

I lay there for a little time, trying to get my breathing under control. Finally I got up onto hands and knees, crawled to where I had a clear view of SupremeCourt below, and reached for the nightscope.

And the rain turned into snow.

The sudden flurry was thick enough to blur the lights below. Wind-hurled flakes stung my face; I felt as cold as I'd ever been in my life. It was an effort to crawl back under an overhang on the rock wall. I huddled there, shivering. Calling Ike on the small handheld device he'd given me would be useless; there was nothing he could do. If the storm went on dumping snow long enough, I'd never make it down and back to the Jeep—I'd freeze to death up here.

I don't know how long I sat there, numb and shaking, my arms wrapped tight around my body. A long time, one of the longest times in my life. I'd about given up hope when the snowfall began to thin, then stopped as suddenly as it had started. The wind abated too, and the night became eerily still. The air cleared, and down below I could once again see the lights of the Harcourt ranch buildings.

Stiffly I moved out from under the overhang and took the scope from its sling. It took a few fumbling tries with my numbed hands to adjust the distance, train it around. Cut back on the focus, cut back again. Finally the Harcourt house came into clear view.

At first all I could see were the cracks in the house's adobe walls. I eased off on the focus a little.

Now I saw window frames. Windows. Figures moving around behind them.

Now a sharper focus, to the maximum.

And then I had it. I snapped the numbers of the planes that were parked within range, then looked through the uncurtained windows.

A crowd of people—mainly men—in formal attire. Waitpersons bustling about with trays of drinks and canapés. The scope was so powerful that I had no trouble spotting individual faces. I located the Old Man, looking surprisingly healthy in spite of his sons' claims of his impending demise. Paul was bustling around, glad-handing the guests. Kurt stood alone to one side; something was not right about his stance...

I located Michael Stein, standing on the fringes of the crowd, watching.

I began photographing again.

After a while there was a pause in the conversations. Men turned. A woman was being ushered ceremoniously into the room. An Indigenous woman, clad in traditional buckskin, her hair in ornately beaded braids.

"Auntie" Mamie Louise.

Mamie Louise looked confused, deep wrinkles riddling her brown skin. Paul hurried forward to greet her, took her hands in his, ushered her to a seat at a small cloth-covered table. The Old Man approached, putting his arm around her narrow shoulders; they spoke for a few moments, and then Paul reappeared, holding what looked like documents and a pen.

A Native in the house of Native haters. There could be only one reason for it.

I took the device Ike had loaned me from my coat pocket, opened it. Ike acknowledged immediately.

"They've got one of the tribal elders there," I told him, "and it looks as if they're getting her to sign papers."

"Forcibly?"

"I can't tell."

Paul was now looming over Mamie Louise, gesturing with his pen at the documents. The Old Man was patting her shoulder. She looked up at them, shaking her head.

I said, "Yes, forcibly."

"Your photographs have reached me. There are two wanted men there. I've got my probable cause, and I've given my people the order to move in."

As I watched the scene below, Kurt's stance shifted. He leaned forward, listening to the exchange among his father, brother, and Mamie Louise. It was growing heated. Mamie Louise repeatedly shook her head. Both men gestured at the documents, and she threw the pen to the floor. Paul slapped her face, and she slipped off her chair, but was on her feet quickly, ready to fight.

Kurt moved then, going up on his toes. Lunged at his brother and father, bringing both of them down and knocking a pistol from Paul's hand.

I heard a crackling from the device in my pocket. Ike's voice came on.

"We've got it under control, McCone."

I continued to photograph the scene through the scope. What I saw was a melee: tangled bodies, flailing fists, angry faces. And FBI agents in their distinctive blue-and-yellow jackets.

"McCone?" Ike's voice. "You okay?"

"Why wouldn't I be? Over and out."

I shut off the device and flopped on my back against the rocky ledge. Barely noticed as loose granite cut into my back. Gunshots and shouts echoed up from the valley.

I ignored everything. After I rested I'd begin the easier climb back down this damn peak.

It would be a long night. The feds would want a statement, and, knowing them, it would have to be a detailed one: How a coalition of rich financiers had discovered the value of Arbritazone and tried to corner the market on properties rich in it. How Paul Harcourt had killed or arranged to have killed, with or without the knowledge of his father and the other profiteers, the two women who had controlled the allotments but refused to make deals. And now that those properties had reverted to the Meruk tribe, how they'd tried to force Mamie Louise to sign them over.

There was more to it than that, I thought, but I wasn't up to figuring it out now. I put the scope back in its case and began the long trek back to the Jeep, praying that the storm had passed and it wouldn't start raining or snowing again.

It didn't.

Reports from Meruk County

The Sisters were happy with the results of my investigation and offered me a bonus. I asked that they donate it to whatever organization they felt needed it most.

Jake Blue has come out of his shell somewhat and is planning a community garden in honor of his sister, Josie.

Sally Bee and Henry Howling Wolf have moved out of Meruk County, to a live-work building for artists in Portland, Oregon.

Ben and Kurt Harcourt, reacting to all the bad publicity, closed their land to Arbritazone seekers and returned to cattle ranching.

Sasha Whitehorse, fully recovered from her ordeal, has realized her dream and escaped to junior college in Sacramento.

The Hogwash Farm is up for sale, its owner having died and the residents having absconded with anything of value.

Jane Ramone is...well, as always, Jane.

Miz Hattie's response to all the commotion was, "Well, I never *heard* of such a thing!"

Mamie Louise vows to keep fighting the good fight for Indigenous tribal rights.

Sheriff Noah Arneson proclaimed upon his arrest for receiving stolen goods, "You can't do this to me! I'm innocent! You can't!"

When told the reason for her daughter's murder, Dorothy Lagomarsino said, "Huh?"

MONDAY, JANUARY 21

3:50 p.m.

"Conference room" usually implies a long polished table, comfortable plush chairs, and a minion providing water and coffee. At M&R our conference room is equipped with an old, scarred round oak table that once graced—or disgraced—the kitchen at All Souls Legal Cooperative, and mismatched chairs scrounged from everywhere over the years. No minions; we carry in our own refreshments.

The table means a lot to some of us. It's a reminder of a simpler time, when the battles we fought were winnable. Now, however, the battles often seem already lost—to greed, stupidity, and out-and-out evil.

Maybe that's why we cling to this hunk of wood with its innocent carvings: "No More Wars!" "HZ Loves AM." "Peace, please!" "Feet off table!" "McCone Rules!" "Doesn't!" "Does too!"

I sat against the wall at the back, listening to Mick do his presentation on the details of the case to the rest of the staff. How Arbritazone could do vast amounts of good but also cause major psychotic breaks in people with long exposure to it. How Paul Harcourt and his father had been determined to corner the market on properties containing large deposits of the mineral and introduce it into the world market. How Paul had become addicted to the drug some years ago, which had led to his accidental strangling of Josie Blue and premeditated murders of Sam Runs Close and Dierdra Two Shoes. His father and brother, to my mind, were equally guilty of his crimes because they had made no effort to control him.

The Harcourts' "special ops boys," Gene Byram and Victor Long, had been paid by Paul to set fire to the shack, but in their confessions they claimed that he hadn't told them I would be inside. They also stated that they'd abducted Sally Bee and Sasha Whitehorse "for kicks." They'll get a different kind of kicks in prison.

I thought about the murdered women. Dierdra Two Shoes: unmarried with no children. Samantha Runs Close: the same. Dierdra and Sam had been approached by the Harcourts about selling their allotments but had turned them down.

In the end it all boiled down to money—money and entitlement.

Mick concluded his presentation, then went on to other cases to be investigated: sexual harassment at a Noe Valley dot-com; a rent dispute in the Haight; garbage wars—again—in Inner Richmond; a suit against the owners of a sweatshop in the Mission.

I liked the kinds of cases that came to us: ones that could make a difference in often powerless people's lives.

I'd asked Mick to chair this conference because, frankly, I didn't have the heart for it. During most of my career these necessary summations had left me feeling empty: someone had suffered, someone had died, the lives of the friends and family of the victim had been diminished. There was satisfaction in bringing the perpetrators to justice, but the cogs in the legal system mesh imperfectly, and often by the time they do—if they do at all—the original outrage has been forgotten.

I looked across the conference table at Hank, who'd decided to drop in for the meeting. His relatively unlined face was at peace, his Brillo-pad hair as wild as ever. He'd pulled me aside when he arrived and told me that he'd decided to remain in the city at least till Habiba went to college.

"Thank you for reading me the riot act," he added.

"That was no riot act. I was merely stating that you should follow your conscience. When I read you the riot act, you'll know it."

I shifted my gaze to my operatives.

Derek Frye, a young Eurasian man with many fashionable tattoos, who had teamed with Mick in various profitable Internet ventures.

Zoe Anderson, a graduate in computer sciences from USC. She hadn't had much experience when she'd come in for an interview, but so far her performance had been exceptional.

Natalie Su, also a recent addition to the team. And a great investigator—she'd actually been able to find two pencil sharpeners that had gone astray in the supply closet.

Ted, his arm in a sling, but unfazed. Surprisingly, he was attired in chinos and a dark-blue sweater. Maybe our fashion plate had finally grown up.

Julia Rafael, who had been on leave for two months, after the death of her sister, who'd been the caregiver for her young son, Antonio. We'd found her a good day care provider and she'd been happy to come back.

Patrick Neilan, a single father, who balanced raising his two sons and his job with outstanding ease.

And I remembered the others whose faces had once greeted me across this table:

Rae, of course—but then, she kept reappearing.

Charlotte Keim, once Mick's love, now married and with a security firm in North Carolina.

Adah Joslyn, good friend and former officer with the SFPD, now in an investigative partnership with Craig Morland, former FBI agent and her husband.

Kendra Williams, who now lives in Washington, D.C., and is an integral part of the Black Lives Matter movement.

Hank and Anne-Marie, of course.

And Hy, frequently.

All of them were members of what we called Team McCone, a bond none of us would ever break. We called each other across the world, from wherever we might be. We commiserated with each other in the bad times, celebrated in the good. We shared photos and news and jokes on the Internet. We enjoyed reunions, usually over some wicked brew.

We were, in the very best sense of the term, a family.

About the Author

Marcia Muller has written many novels and short stories. She has won six Anthony Awards and a Shamus Award and is also the recipient of the Private Eye Writers of America Lifetime Achievement Award as well as the Mystery Writers of America Grand Master Award, the organization's highest accolade. She lives in northern California with her husband, mystery writer Bill Pronzini.

LOOKING FOR MORE
SHARON McCONE?

TURN THE PAGE FOR
A PREVIEW OF
MARCIA MULLER'S
THE BREAKERS.

AVAILABLE NOW

SATURDAY, AUGUST 6

1:27 p.m.

The southwestern part of San Francisco, where the Pacific washes upon Ocean Beach, is known by long-term residents as the Outerlands, or Out There by the Beach. Where surf meets sand, impenetrable fog frequently flows in, making the horns under the Golden Gate Bridge moan dolefully. The average temperature is in the midfifties—chilly at best—and fast-moving riptides are a hazard that have caused a number of experienced swimmers and surfers to be swept away and drowned. Still, the swimmers and surfers persist, refusing to allow the sea to prevail.

Above the beach, the Great Highway slices north and south, separating the dunes from the houses on Forty-Eighth Avenue in the Outer Sunset district. By and large, the homes there are small but well-kept, except for the occasional monstrosity—a fully rigged pirate ship or a model of the *Santa María* that rears its ugly head as if its builders had been trying to make a statement.

About what? I've often wondered. I've never been able to figure that one out.

I arrived at the building called the Breakers, on El Jardin de la Playa—the Garden of the Beach, although most locals simply call it Jardin Street—twenty minutes early for my appointment with a man called Zack Kaplan, who wanted to show me something "truly bizarre."

"Run-down" would be a better term to describe the place than "bizarre." The Breakers was undistinguished to say the least: gray aluminum siding blistered by the sea winds; a roof that was shedding its shingles; sliding aluminum-sash windows that were too tiny and high up to take advantage of the sea view. The ground around it was gravel, mostly washed away to mud; there were no trees or shrubs or anything that pretended to be landscaping.

Instead of waiting in my car, I decided to stretch my legs. The weather was overcast, windy, so I zipped my jacket higher. Then I walked down to the Beach Chalet Brewery and Restaurant and crossed the highway to stand at the seawall, salt spray and sand peppering my face, looking out at the waves and a few hardy souls walking along the beach.

I'd set the appointment with Zack Kaplan at the request of my former neighbors and friends Trish and Jim Curley. They were vacationing in Costa Rica and neither they nor their son, Sean, had been able to contact their daughter, Michelle (Chelle to her friends) on her cell, her computer, or the phone at the Breakers, the building she was currently rehabbing. Zack Kaplan was one of the two remaining tenants, and he hadn't been able to reach her either.

Chelle, at twenty-three, was an up-and-coming restorer of old buildings and very conscientious; no way she would leave her cell off or fail to respond to a call from her parents. Would I check on her? Trish had asked.

Chelle was one of my favorite people. When I'd first moved next door to her family, she'd volunteered to bring in packages and feed my cats during my frequent absences; later, in a period when I couldn't drive, she'd been my chauffeur; she'd even helped on a couple of my cases, until her parents had found out and forbidden her the joys of private investigation. She was smart, innovative, and always there for those who needed her. I wanted this to be one time I was there for her.

At five minutes to two I walked back to the Breakers. Three minutes more passed, and then a battered olive-drab Jeep pulled up. A man in jeans and a thick wool shirt got out and came toward me.

"Ms. McCone?" he said. "I'm Zack Kaplan."

Kaplan had a narrow, bearded face and friendly brown eyes. Black hair stuck out from under his knitted ski cap. He wasn't tall—only a couple of inches over my own five-foot-six—but I sensed a strength in his wiry body.

We shook hands. "I see you found the building all right," he said. "Pretty grim, huh? But when I moved in, it was all I could afford. Now I'm in the grips of lethargy."

That building would make me lethargic too.

I asked, "Still no word from Chelle?"

"No, nothing. I'm starting to get alarmed."

"Me too. I understand Chelle is both rehabbing and living here."

"Yeah. Personally, I think she's nuts."

In a way I did too. But Chelle really got into her work, and described living in a derelict building as a way of "getting at its soul."

"She have anybody there with her?" Chelle sometimes asked her current boyfriend to stay with her and pitch in.

"A guy named Damon for a week or so, but he split."

"Are you and she...?"

"No, we're just friends. My life's complicated enough without romance entering the picture."

"So you've known her how long?"

"Just since she moved in in May."

"Has she made much progress on the rehab?"

Zack looked troubled. "Not much. First there was Damon, who broke more stuff than he fixed. Next Al Majewski and Ollie Morse. They're good workers, had been on the crew of one of her other jobs in the past. But if she doesn't show up and give them their back pay, they'll have to look for other employment."

"Stop a minute—who's Damon?"

"I never did get his last name. He and Chelle had a thing going, but not for very long. Damon started telling her lies about Al and Ollie stealing from her. But she found out otherwise and gave him the ax."

"Do you know where I can find him?"

"No idea." Zack sighed. "I don't know what's

going to happen to the place. The owner gave Chelle a long escrow, until she could get her final payment from her last rehab job, but it's due to close next Friday. The electric and water bills are overdue. I paid some of them—after all, I'm the only one using the utilities—but I'm a student at SF State, and I can't keep it up indefinitely."

"You said on the phone it's been a week since you've seen Chelle?"

"A week ago tomorrow. Last Sunday."

"She gave you no indication that she was planning on taking a trip? Visiting a friend or family?"

"No."

"What did she take with her? For instance, clothes for a warm or a cool climate?"

"Nothing."

This was bad—Chelle loved clothes, and her wardrobe, while sometimes eccentric, was stunning.

Zack added, "Her laptop and cell are gone, her backpack, money, and ID too."

"Well," I said, more heartily than I felt, "let's see what we can find out."

As we walked over to the building, Zack asked, "You're a licensed PI, right?"

"Yes." I handed him one of my cards.

"That kind of exciting work fascinates me."

"It's not as exciting as books and film make it seem."

"But still, unraveling the circumstances of crimes, getting at the truth, seeing that the bad guys get theirs…"

"Sitting on your butt during long stakeouts, dealing with difficult clients, and writing reports too."

"Every job's got its drawbacks."

"Let's go inside and check Chelle's apartment."

"Uh, it's not really an apartment."

"What is it, then?"

"You'll see."

The interior of the building was musty—the smell a combination of stale sea air, mildew, and dust. We entered by what Zack called the lobby, although there was no reception desk, furnishings, or tenant mailboxes. The walls were faded beige, and the worn carpeting had once been vivid with the bright pink, red, and yellow of overblown daisies. The flowers were faded now, their petals begrimed.

Zack whispered, "Like I said, pretty grim."

"Why are you whispering?"

He shrugged. "When I come in by this part of the building it has that effect on me. Like I don't want to wake anybody—or any*thing*—up."

A stairway—partially collapsed—rose to the second floor, a long first-floor hallway to the left of it. Zack led me to a door halfway along the hall and pushed it open. Inside was what looked to be an ordinary living room containing only a few mismatched and worn pieces of furniture. I frowned.

Zack noticed my look and said, "In the bedroom."

The bedroom was empty except for a sturdy stepladder that stood in its middle. Above it was an open trapdoor. "I'll go first," Zack said, "and give you a pull up."

In a few quick steps he disappeared through the trapdoor. A blazing light came on up there. I started up the ladder and he helped me climb through the hole.

An entire low-ceilinged room existed there between the two floors. I blinked against the harsh light and looked around.

"This building was a nightclub, cathouse, and bar all through Prohibition and up to 1944," Zack said. "The elite of the city flocked here, but then it went out of style. The building was sold and resold, but none of the owners could revive the nightclub trade, and thirty years ago one of them chopped it up into apartments. He didn't bother to renovate this floor because providing access would be too expensive. There used to be stairs, but vandals tore them out. This is where Chelle's been sleeping." He led me to a nook between two heavy support beams where a sleeping bag and fluffy pillows rested on an air mattress.

Chelle might have been camping out here, but she was doing it in style: a coffee machine was plugged into a nearby outlet; a small TV sat on a table at the foot of the bed; her clothes, in bright colors and exotic materials, hung on a pole. I fingered a cape trimmed with beaded braid that I particularly liked.

"Well," I said after a moment, "this place doesn't look so bad."

"Not this part, no." There was a dark note in Zack's voice. "But look over here." He went about six feet away and moved aside a Japanese screen that I recognized as having been in Chelle's bedroom at her parents' house on Church Street. What it revealed made me recoil.

The wall there was covered with old wanted posters, artists' renderings, photographs, and newspaper articles on some of the worst mass murderers in

California's history. Jack the Ripper had never set foot in the state, I hoped, but you couldn't have a wall of horrors without him. The drawing wasn't a good one, but what could anybody do with a subject who had never been seen? Other killers, most of them from the past few decades, carried out the ugly theme: The Zodiac and Zebra killers of the 1970s. Charles Manson and his girls. Dan White, who in 1978 assassinated Mayor George Moscone and Supervisor Harvey Milk. Jim Jones, who in the same year led more than nine hundred of his Peoples Temple followers to commit suicide at their compound in Guyana. The godfather of the Oakland drug trade, Felix Mitchell, who was lionized at his 1986 funeral. Gian Luigi Ferri, the 101 California Street shooter. Scott Peterson, now under death sentence for the 2002 Christmas Eve killing of his wife, Laci, and their unborn child, whose bodies he had then dumped into San Francisco Bay.

I shuddered. "How could Chelle live with this?"

He shrugged. "The reason for the screen."

"But she had to know it was there."

"Some of us are braver than others, I guess."

"She certainly didn't assemble the wall."

"God, no. It's been here for a long time—since before I moved into the building, anyway."

"Then who did?"

"Don't know. This unit had been empty for a while when Chelle took it over."

And now Chelle's gone missing.

I said, "My firm will take over payment of the utilities till her parents decide what to do. I'll need the name of the person Chelle's buying it from."

"That's easy—it's Cap'n Bobby. He runs a fish taco shop a couple of blocks away."

"Thanks, Zack. And thanks for your time and information."

"No worries. I'm with you—all I want is Chelle safely back here."

I thought, *A good man*, if *he's been completely honest with me.*